A Single Rook

by

Janet Ollerenshaw

Dedication

This work is dedicated to all the wonderful staff at
Addenbrookes Hospital, Cambridge without whom
I may never have completed this sixth book.

Acknowledgments

My grateful thanks go to Darin, my patient agent;

To my daughter Megan for her excellent proof-reading expertise;

To my long suffering mother who never fails to praise my efforts;

And to Mark who is always encouraging me and is enthusiastic in his suggestions of new ideas,

"You could write a book about that...!" – Perhaps I will!

Lastly, to you my reader(s) – Thank you for taking a chance on me!

A single rook is a certain crow;
but rows of crows,
despite their looks,
are rooks!

Chapter 1

The injured bird flapped feebly and hobbled to the edge of the crumbling tarmac road. On hearing an approaching motor, other younger and healthier looking specimens kept their distance and flew swiftly up into the ice blue sky, where they circled and cawed as the vehicle came to a stop nearby. A young man left the warmth of his cab and hurried carefully towards the invalid creature. As he drew near, the black bird struggled to get further away from perceived danger and potential capture. It squawked and again flapped wildly but could not lift up from the muddied field. Taking off his jacket, he threw it gently over the bird; wary of beak and claws with which it might make a last-minute effort to escape his attempts to bring it some comfort.

Scooping the bundle up into his arms, he made his way quietly back to the pick-up and placed his find on the passenger seat before sliding once more behind the wheel and continuing on his way home.

Home was an unremarkable canal boat, moored in the furthest corner of a large marina. It was painted dark green with little evidence of its former glory and traditional bright decoration. The rear cockpit was covered with a tatty tarpaulin which flapped in the light wind that lifted Kevin's floppy fringe from his brow. Unhooking the corner from a strategically placed cleat, he stepped down into the cockpit well and, taking a key from his back pocket, unlocked the cabin doors.

Inside the long narrow vessel was surprisingly warm and tidy, despite it appearing to be overfull. Tidy, that is if you're prepared to ignore the various bits of paraphernalia that were strewn on the bed in the tiny chamber and the marginally better organised tools and equipment that hung from a row of hooks affixed to the side wall opposite a sliding door. The door had obviously not been closed for a long time and there was no evidence at all of the bed having been used for its intended purpose. There was no mattress and no bedding, just boards and cupboards above the head and foot. The cupboards were closed although small pieces of fabric showed here and there making it clear that there was plenty stored within.

Further into the boat the space opened out into a galley kitchen and a dining area at the far end of which was a wood burning stove with a tall chimney that protruded through the ceiling. Here then was the source of the warmth. A kettle sang on the top of the stove and from elsewhere emanated a delicious aroma – a stew or casserole perhaps – which had been left to cook while Kevin was out doing his business.

His business; what exactly was his business? From the various chisels, saws, axes and rasps that hung from the aforementioned hooks, you might imagine that he was some sort of carpenter and indeed he had fitted out most of the interior of his boat. As you look around it becomes apparent from the sleeping bag neatly rolled up on the end of the dining bench, that this was where Kevin slept – and ate, and worked on his small laptop. Perhaps he watched Netflix or listened to music, or maybe he just enjoyed the peace and quiet of his compact home afloat.

A short while later the ailing bird was comfortably ensconced in a large dog cage which Kevin, having retrieved it from under some other items on the disused bed, had unfolded, placed towels inside and then situated it in the space opposite his bench-come-bed-come everything else. The bird eyed him warily as he made himself a cup of coffee and ladled himself a bowl of steaming stew from the big iron pot that stood on his small Calor gas stove.

It was obvious from his calculated movements that this was a routine that he followed on a regular basis. Soon he was dozing in front of a blank screened laptop. He had intended to check his emails to see if there were any new orders and to make a note of his bank balance, but tiredness overcame him. He forced himself up from the seat, found a bowl for water for the bird and another for some wild bird seed that he happened to have in his store cupboard above the small fridge, placed a good-sized log in the stove and was just unrolling his sleeping bag when there was a loud knock on the roof above his head.

***

Standing on the outer edge of a large group of people or sitting in the far corner of a crowded room; waiting alone at the end of a line of queuing participants or deliberately choosing to be the one for whom there was no room in whichever particular mode of transport was being offered, he had always felt himself to be different – not special, not privileged or ignored, just not the same as everyone else. He grew up with just his mum who had been almost as insular as he had become. She had few friends, no husband, no siblings and only her grandmother who had cared for her since her parents died when she was just twelve years old. Don't misunderstand me – they were not unhappy and had no issue with other people but they just didn't need anyone else.

Of course, Kevin had toyed with the idea of romance – what young man has not? Perhaps it would have been nice to live in a normal house with a wife and children, a cat or a dog and a nine-to-five job to pay the bills. A holiday abroad once a year maybe or at least a week by the sea – he had always loved the water – but in the end, it was not to be and he couldn't say that he regretted anything. When his mother died – throat cancer can be the cruellest of afflictions – he was sad but relieved that she no longer had to suffer the indignities of incapacitation. He could tell from the look in her eyes that she hated her imposed reliance on other people and greatly preferred that he did as much of the caring as he could. Inevitably there were some procedures and necessities that were beyond his abilities and for those, home nurses attended her in her final few months.

After the funeral he found himself more alone than he had ever been. He consulted with the bank manager, a solicitor and an estate agent only to discover that there was very little equity in the house and no money to speak of in the bank. So it was that the house was sold and his mother's possessions mostly given to charity although he took enough to furnish his home afloat which was the best option he could afford and in which he found himself inordinately happy and comfortable. There were tuts and looks of disapproval from a few of his mother's neighbours but he shrugged them off, thanked them politely for their offers of help (not that there had been much of that) and waved them goodbye. As he rumbled away in the shabby pickup, piled high with the paraphernalia needed to kit out his new home, he had breathed a huge sigh of relief that it was all over and done with.

The marina, where we found Kevin's boat tucked away, is on the outskirts of a small town. There is easy access to shops and facilities and even easier access to the river. In the summer months the river is busy with holiday makers, day trippers, anglers, dog walkers and cyclists on the tow-paths and other people who just want to admire or cast a critical eye over the various floating craft. Although

Kevin did not enjoy the busier times and the proximity of so many people, it was the needs and desires of these owners and visitors that provided him with an income.

Chapter 2

Tall, thin and wiry, of an indeterminate age, she gazed into the water trying to decide what exactly she was seeing half submerged in the murky depths. It had been the desperate mewing of a cat that had first alerted her as she made her careful way back along the towpath toward the cabin, she and her sister called home. Unbeknownst to her, everyone referred to her as Pork-pie because of the hat she habitually wore perched on the top of her extremely short hair. Despite its clipped length, wisps insisted on escaping from under the hat which resembled a fez only shorter and without a tassel; its dull brown shade making it even more like the pie of her nickname.

She peered further into the river and was in danger of toppling in when, with a cry of alarm, she recognised what looked like a hand as the thing, whatever it was, stirred slightly in the weak current. Her own hand flew to her mouth as she turned, almost tripped over the now pacified cat which was entwining itself lovingly around her legs, and scrambled up the bank as she realised that this was something with which she was going to need help.

It was no good going home to the cabin to fetch her sister who was never any use in any type of emergency; all she ever did in such situations was to flap and panic. No, she would go to Kevin, that really helpful young man who kept himself to himself but who could be relied upon to help out in most awkward situations. Thus, it was that it was she who provided the aforementioned thump on the cabin roof of Kevin's boat.

"Please come – now!" the urgency in his visitor's voice was obvious and so Kevin, not stopping to put clothes on over his pyjamas into which he had only just changed, grabbed his overcoat and wellingtons as he hurried up the gangway steps and out into the cockpit. Before he had a chance to open his mouth and question his summons, Pork-pie retorted, "No need to bother with waterproofs, you're going to get wet anyway! I should take everything off if I were you!" Not waiting for a response, she commanded him to, "come on," and hurried back down the way she had come.

Kevin reached for a boat hook and a length of rope as he quickly followed the authoritative lady the hundred yards or so to where he found her pointing into the water. The abovementioned cat had not left the spot, making it easy for Pork-pie to relocate the floating object she had noticed on her first journey home past this spot. The 'thing', whatever it was, had moved a little and was further away from the bank than when first seen and since it was perfectly obvious what action was required, neither Kevin nor Pork-pie spoke as Kevin first tried to reach the bundle with the boat hook and on finding it too far away, then took the rope and plunged feet first into the rather cold water. His wellingtons immediately filled with water but he was able to wade out far enough to throw a coil of rope around the nearest part of the floating object and pulled it slowly towards him.

It gently rolled over and, with a gasp, Kevin realised that he was looking down into the face of a child. Surely it must be dead? It had been at least five minutes since Pork-pie had banged on his roof and he had absolutely no idea how long the child had been in the water before Pork-pie had first noticed it. Nevertheless, he carried the sopping bundle out onto the bank and turning it face down, began to use the Holger-Neilson lifesaving techniques he had learned long ago at school.

Pork-pie stood silently watching him; her face as white as chalk and her thin body shaking a little both with cold and with shock at what she was witnessing. Much to their mutual astonishment, after several minutes, the little body gave an involuntary gasp and water gushed out of its mouth as it choked and gave a weak cry. Still without speaking, Pork-pie took off her coat and gave it to Kevin to wrap around the small person.

What to do now, they both wondered; police or ambulance; both or neither? Why would there be any question you might wonder, but both rescuers much preferred their own company and resources and were wary of outside help, be it official or friendly; hence the reluctance to involve any officialdom. For a few moments they stared at each other, the older lady and the reclusive younger man, as they wordlessly communicated. The child could not be taken to Pork-pie's cabin without alerting her sister who would undoubtedly want to involve every possible service, including the local media. As different as chalk and cheese, Beanie (you can guess the derivation of her nickname) was garrulous, nosy and served as the marina's gossip in complete contrast to Pork-pie's preference for isolation and anonymity.

No, the cabin was not the solution. That left Kevin's boat as the only other viable option, at least for the time being; perhaps until the child could reveal its identity and how it came to be floating in the river. As far as the saviours knew, there had been no local reports of a missing child and if it was a national issue, they would surely hear about it before long. However, that would not be before the next day since neither watched television and relied on newspapers and hearsay for national events and occurrences, and something needed to be done right now.

Kevin, squelching in his own water-logged wellingtons and dripping pyjama bottoms, carried the soggy bundle back to his cosy boat. The log he had left in the stove was burning steadily and the small space was toasty warm. He placed the child on his unrolled sleeping bag and found towels with which to dry as best he could. Pork-pie, having followed him uncertainly, stood back and watched as he carefully removed the sodden outer clothes, revealing a skinny girl of uncertain age. As he gently dried her skin, her eyes remained closed but her chest rose and fell as she breathed steadily and Kevin felt certain that she would survive the night without any further medical attention.

Whether she had suffered any brain damage from lack of oxygen, or respiratory problems from the ingress of water to her lungs, he would not be able to determine until time had passed. Not having a ready supply of female clothing, he fetched a T-shirt of his own in which to clothe her as he settled her in his sleeping bag for the night. He offered Pork-pie some of the stew he had eaten from earlier, but she politely refused and said that she should get back to her sister who might be wondering where she had been all this time. She left as quietly as she had come but with the promise of a further visit in the morning.

Kevin gazed down at the sleeping child before finding himself some dry clothes, a pillow and a blanket into which he wrapped himself as he lay down on the floor between the bench and the dog-come-bird cage. Surprisingly, in no time at all he was fast asleep and all was quiet apart from the occasional rustle from the cage and the gentle snores of three sleeping forms; one on the bench, another on the floor and a third, the small cat that had crept in unseen as the tall lady let herself out and who had curled herself discreetly by the feet of the unfortunate child.

Chapter 3

Staring blankly at the plain white wall, unseeing of the shadows that flitted across the sunlit canvas, unfeeling of the cool breeze that crept in through the small fanlight window that was always ajar no matter what external temperature prevailed, she hugged herself more tightly and sighed for the umpteenth time. The exhaled breath was dissipated quickly by the aforementioned breeze but not before she idly noted that it curled and swirled like cigarette smoke before disappearing into the ether. She supposed she ought to be doing something... something other than sitting here day after day pondering on... what? Was she pondering? Was she thinking of anything at all? She couldn't even raise an answer to either of those passing thoughts – the effort was just too much. And so, as usual, she simply lay back down on the bed, pulled the coverlet right over her head and sank back into the oblivion of dreamless nothingness that she couldn't even call sleep...

It was some time later when she was aroused by persistent loud rapping on her door, alternated with shouts and overlong pressings of the electric buzzer. She stumbled out of bed, ran her fingers ineffectually through her tousled hair and, dragging the tattered blanket around her shoulders, stumbled down the stairs to answer the summons. Her astonishment at the sight of two smartly dressed and clip-boarded strangers standing impatiently on her doorstep was only tempered by her irritation at the crowd of curious passers-by who craned their necks to see whatever local drama was unfolding.

Before she could collect herself sufficiently to speak in order to enquire what was wanted of her, the woman asked, "May we come in? We need to speak to you."

Without replying, Carol simply pushed the door further open and led the way to her small, untidy lounge. She shoved the accumulated detritus to one side and plonked herself down in the middle of the sagging settee, leaving no doubt that she did not intend to make room for anyone else. That meant that one visistor, the female, perched on the edge of the single dining chair which occupied the only other sitting space, near the front window, whilst the other, a burly but not unkind looking man, stood and leant uncomfortably against the doorpost.

Despite it being mid-March, a shabby Christmas tree stood next to the hearth. Complete with baubles and tinsel, it looked incongruous and anything but festive as its former glory was now festooned with cobwebs and dust. Round its base were placed unopened packages in what were once gaudy wrappings. Wendy Crispin found herself wondering who the packages were for and what greetings the now almost illegible labels carried.

Realising the need for some sort of acknowledgement of her unexpected, and to be honest, unwanted guests, Carol muttered, "Would you like coffee?" followed by a gruff, "there's no milk though..." She trailed off before adding that there was no sugar either but neither visitor accepted her offer before briskly diving in to the reason for their visit.

***

After they had gone, and with her thoughts swirling enough to make her feel quite dizzy, Carol sat where they had left her in the middle of the sofa. Surrounded by piles of indeterminate junk, she looked mournfully at the seemingly insurmountable task of clearing it all away. Audibly sighing, she did what she had been doing for the last months – ever since it had happened – pulled the blanket over her head and rocked to and fro, before laying down on top of the paper-strewn cushions and closed her eyes and her mind to what she knew she ought to be doing.

***

No matter how hard she tried to block out the memories of that terrible time, they insisted on creeping inexorably into her heart and leaking from her eyes. Always accompanied by unanswerable questions, they left her totally incapacitated, empty yet full, angry yet deeply sorrowful, longing for closure and escape from the all-encompassing

19

misery and yet desperate to cling onto the very memories that tormented her. There was no escape; there was no future, there was nothing to live for... and yet... perhaps she had been offered a life-line? Someone needed her? How could that be? Why... who... when? What had the woman said about next week?

Carol roused herself sufficiently to sit up again in an attempt to make sense of what had been asked of her. She reached for the small sheaf of papers that Wendy Crispin had placed carefully on the chair she had vacated on conclusion of the visit. Skimming swiftly down the pages she found the telephone number she was looking for and, for the first time in months, she made a decision to do something positive. She would read the papers more carefully and make a note of questions to ask. Then she would make the call to find out more about what was wanted of her.

Unsurprisingly, to those of us who are not weighed down by the black dog of depression, she felt much better and even slightly energised by the thought of having something positive on which to focus. Nevertheless, even the effort of thinking was exhausting and she barely found the energy to make her way to the kitchen in order to make a milk-less and unsweetened coffee.

Glancing at her reflection in the dusty hall mirror as she returned to the sofa with the hot coffee, she noted the sallow skin and tangled hair of the shabby figure staring back at her. Perhaps a bath or shower was necessary? She hadn't even considered her personal hygiene for a long time – what must the officers have thought of her? Suddenly, and with something of a shock, she acknowledged that she had begun to emerge from the terrible depths of despair that had been her refuge and penance for far too long.

Chapter 4

For a few moments, Kevin was confused as he drifted between sleep and wakefulness. There were unusual sounds filtering through into his sleep-befuddled ears and a slightly unpleasant aroma of something burning. However, the sound that eventually had him sitting bolt upright was a peal of laughter following a raucous cawing. Instantly he remembered; the girl, the bird... and a cat? The vision that met his now wide-awake eyes was not one that he had ever expected to witness in his cramped living quarters. A tousle-headed child, wrapped in his sleeping bag, was kneeling on the floor and watching as a small grey cat delicately pushed its paw through the bars of his dog cage and swiped ineffectively at a rather angry black feathered bird. Beak and claws jabbed at each other, but neither quite able to reach the other. Each time the cat struck out, the bird flapped, jabbed and cawed and the child laughed delightedly.

The laughter stopped abruptly as Kevin's deep voice interrupted the game; "Don't!" he roared and all three creatures froze in mid action. After a few seconds complete silence, the child disappeared into the folds of its quilted cloak, the cat shot out of range and cowered behind the kitchen waste bin and the bird scuttled to the back of the cage. Realising the inappropriateness of his introduction to all three guests, he cleared his throat and muttered, "Sorry, but you were frightening the bird. They are sensitive creatures and can die from fright. Please come out, I know you didn't mean any harm and I'm not angry, I won't hurt you," and, after a pause, "Are you hungry? Would you like some breakfast?"

Not looking toward the still hidden child, Kevin stood up, stretching a little as he eased his somewhat cramped muscles into action, and made his way to the galley kitchen. He was greeted by a mess of extraordinary proportions! The lid of his stew-pot had been pushed aside and a ladle inserted, presumably to extract some of the contents. But instead of a dirty bowl and spoon, there was only copious amounts of food dripped onto the still burning calor gas hob – which explained the burning aroma that had assailed his nostrils. On the drainer and floor were feline footprints liberally sprinkled wherever the cat had sprung after filling its belly directly from the pot and scrunched up on the worktop were his dishcloth and tea-towel, both equally well decorated with globs of food and soaked in gravy. It was apparent that both child and cat had already helped themselves to breakfast.

In his usual stoic manner, Kevin began silently to clear up the mayhem and gradually as he worked, two perpetrators emerged from their hiding places. Rattling from the cage evidenced the bird's restored equilibrium and soon three pairs of eyes watched him as he made himself a strong coffee and a slice of toast spread liberally with butter and marmalade.

What to do with this mini-invasion of his preferred privacy? He was no longer concerned that the child had suffered unduly from its soggy experience of the previous day. Nevertheless, surely, she must belong to someone, somewhere; a someone who was no doubt frantically looking for this waif. He realised with a start that he hadn't checked the local news reports and was about to turn on the radio when another sharp rap on his rooftop announced the arrival of Pork-pie who entered without waiting for permission and plonked a pile of newspapers on top of the dog-cum-bird cage. Without preamble she declared that there was nothing in any of those about a missing child, that she'd checked the news reports on breakfast television and had even ventured to ask her sister to look on social media (which was, in any case, her regular morning ritual) to see if anything had been mentioned. Ignoring her mild surprise at the request, Beanie had scrutinised the screen for a little longer than usual but... Nothing. Not a word. Absolutely no indication that anyone had lost anyone or anything!

So, what to do?

The obvious first move would be to inform the police but for some inexplicable reason Kevin found himself reluctant to do that. He seemed to sense that here was something deeper and more complicated than simply a missing or runaway child and that there had been some greater purpose in his involvement in whatever was unfolding through this experience. He sighed deeply, thanked Pork-pie for her help, wordlessly handed her a steaming mug of coffee and began to tidy the blanket and sleeping bag away. He folded them neatly and placed them carefully in the locker beneath the bench together with the extra pillow and towels from the night before. And all the time he was watched by four pairs of wary eyes; the cat's half-closed amber eyes as she lay curled in the girl's arms, blinking and staring through lowered lashes, the bird with its head on one side and Pork-pie alternately sipping her coffee and gazing at him over the rim of the mug.

Eventually he cleared his throat as if preparing for speech but instead a prolonged sigh emanated from between his lips before he said, "Your name! What's your name?"

Pork-pie looked up in surprise and, "Mary," she replied, and then, "Oh! Not me, of course, how silly. Don't tell anyone that will you?" A wry and shy grin flitted across her wrinkled face before she leant towards the bowed, curly head of the child saying, "It's your name we need to know child! What are you called?" There was a drawn-out pause before the child whispered, "Brat, Nuisance, Pain-in-my-ass, Thingamy and sometimes Sophie. Depends who is calling me."

The two adults looked towards each other with expressions of surprise and concern alternating on their faces as they took in and processed the insinuation behind the child's words. Clearly, she had belonged to someone or even some-ones but there seemed to be a significant question over whether that belonging had been valued in any way.

Pork-pie cleared her throat and turned away as she brushed a tear from her cheek before declaring in an overly bright tone, "Well, I think I shall call you Sophie, if that's alright with you?"

"Me too," muttered Kevin gruffly and both were rewarded with a bright smile as the child stood up abruptly, depositing the cat unceremoniously on the floor, and threw her arms around first Kevin and then Pork-pie.

"Can I stay here?" came the muffled request as she buried her face in Pork-pie's old coat.

Chapter 5

The stench that assailed his nostrils as he surfaced slowly from his alcohol-imposed stupor, was significantly worse than usual. Unwashed body odour, vomit, used plates and cutlery, burnt cooking pots and overfull ash trays he was used to, but this was something more and he couldn't immediately identify its awfulness. Struggling to his feet, he picked his way across the room and, avoiding the accumulated detritus, reached the kitchen door. His goal was coffee; strong, hot and sweet, to counter the excesses of the previous days and to stimulate his ever-flagging energies into some degree of motivation in order to address this new problem.

He never made it to the kettle, let alone the coffee jar. The sight that greeted him was horrendous; something straight out of one of those cheap horror films that he used to watch in his youth. To begin with, he thought he was still dreaming but after first pinching himself and then drawing a deep breath – which he instantly regretted as the stink that had only affected his nose, now penetrated his lungs and he coughed, spluttered and retched before throwing open the kitchen window to alleviate the awfulness.

Everywhere was littered with foodstuffs; as though someone had ransacked the cupboards and emptied every conceivable ingredient straight onto the floor. However, bad enough in itself, this was not the worst. In the middle of the mess, lying in an enormous pool of blood, was a body – a very dead body.

To begin with, he was reluctant to get near enough to identify who was spread-eagled on his kitchen floor. His first instinct was to run; to shout, to cry for help or simply to get away from this horrible thing that didn't seem to bear any relation to his reality. But real it was and the realisation jolted him from his hung-over daze and enabled him to creep closer to the recumbent figure. 'Female' he registered as he observed the long hair and painted fingernails. 'Dead' – well that was pretty obvious; he chided himself; 'Smelly,' as he retched again and stepped carefully over the body in order to open the back door.

What to do? Now it may seem obvious to you or me that the first thing to do would be to phone the police. However, firstly he had mislaid his mobile phone; secondly, he didn't have the best of relationships with the local constabulary; thirdly, he had absolutely no idea where he had spent the last few days and, fourthly, he knew very well who the dead person was. All of which could all too easily combine to put him in first position as suspect; a position he had no intention of occupying. The one thing of which he was absolutely certain was that he had not killed his wife.

He supposed he ought to feel something; horror, sorrow, shock – anything really. But truth to tell he was numb from head to toe; he didn't feel anything other than a slight sense of the unreal. He was dreaming, sleepwalking, he would wake up soon and all would be normal. He couldn't make himself go back into the kitchen so he took himself down the road to the local pub where a beer would suffice in place of the missed coffee.

Sometime later he could be found perched on a bar-stool, a row of empty glasses in front of his unconscious head as he slept on his folded arms whilst the disgruntled barmaid wiped the surfaces around his tousled and aromatic form as she wondered whether she should wake him and ask him to leave before the midday lunch customers arrived.

***

The back door was ajar. The three children paused uncertainly on the grimy doorstep.

"Phaw!" gasped Billy, "What a stink!"

"Smells like something died in there!" agreed Frankie, little realising how close to the truth his analysis was.

"I wanna go home," whined Winnie, "I don' like it an it's tre'passin'. Mum said..." but she trailed off leaving what Mum said unspoken as Billy lashed out with both his hand and his words, "Go home then stupid. I didn't wanna bring you anyways. Mum said I had to!"

"Then I can't go home, can I?" Winnie opined as she began to cry, "Mum said you had to look after me 'cos she was goin' out for a bit."

The argument came to an abrupt halt as a screech emanated from the kitchen and Frankie, who had tired of waiting for his friends to decide what to do, came hurtling out of the kitchen door. His eyes were wide and wild, his face as pale as chalk and his words utterly incoherent. "Gotta get out of 'ere." he gasped, "Come on," and he grabbed Winnie's hand, pushed Billy with a fist in the small of his back and propelled him and dragged the girl back down the garden path. He didn't stop pushing and pulling until they reached the small playground on the opposite corner of the main road.

With no breath left for crying or speaking, there were a few minutes silence as the threesome sat on the grass and stared at each other.

"What was all that..."

"We ain't never going back..."

"I want my Mu..."

...all three spoke at once and all three left unfinished sentences hanging in a further brief silence.

Frankie spoke first, "There's a woman lying on the floor and loads of blood and mess everywhere," he explained. Billy gasped and Winnie began to cry again. "Stop that blubberin'." Billy was truly fed up with dragging his cry-baby sister everywhere. He'd be heartily glad when she was old enough to be left on her own. "I s'pose we ought to tell someone what we seen..." he continued uncertainly. However, that prospect posed something of a problem given that they almost certainly shouldn't have been in the garden of that house; let alone looking or going into the kitchen. However, ingenuity stepped in and he announced, "Well, I didn't go in did I? It was you what saw it, so you could've told me and I can tell the coppers 'cos I'm innocent aren't I?"

Frankie pondered the idea for a few minutes and then he nodded slowly, "you'll 'ave to shut 'er up," as he glared pointedly at the still sobbing Winnie, "but I can go round my mate's house and you don't 'ave to say it were me what saw the... you know what," he trailed off... and then added, "It oughta be okay. After all we didn't actually do anything bad except for looking in." And after a further pause, and for all his usual bravado, he added quietly, "I wish I 'adn't!"

Thus, it was agreed and a short time later, Billie and a still tearful Winnie were sitting in a small interview room at the local police station while they waited, firstly, for their mother to arrive and secondly, for the nice female police lady, who had given them squash and biscuits, to come back to talk to them...

Chapter 6

Kevin sat, head bowed and stared disconsolately at his hands as he absent-mindedly twiddled and intertwined his fingers. It was chilly and unwelcoming in the reception area and the chairs were hard and uncompromising. He had already waited for quite some time and had watched several other people come and go. He was extremely uncomfortable in this environment – in fact he was uncomfortable in almost any place that wasn't his boat, outside or working on some project, either paid or voluntary. Sitting and waiting was not something that he did. However, wait he must...

He had already been in the police station long enough to be fidgety when the two young children entered. Their heads close together and a conspiratorial air about them, he wondered idly why they were there, but wasn't sufficiently interested to give them more than a passing thought. Nevertheless, the older boy's impatience with the sniffles emanating from the smaller, presumably younger, girl, struck him as being in stark contrast with the poise and composure of Sophie.

After much deliberation, and in discussion with Pork-pie, it had eventually been decided that he should report their find to the police. It was quite probable that her absence hadn't been noticed by those who should have been caring for her, given that there didn't seem to have been a lot of care received by the young girl. She was ridiculously grateful for even the smallest gesture of kindness and was effusive and generous in her thanks. Despite her shy independence and her determination to look after herself, she gave hugs freely and Kevin was left in no doubt at all that here was a child who was used to more unkindness than loving but who, consequently, had learned to be stoically self-assured.

What he really didn't want to happen was the interference of Social Services who would undoubtedly think his circumstances unsuitable for a young child. After all, a single male, living on a boat and with no experience whatsoever of looking after a child, he didn't exactly present as an ideal foster parent. Accordingly, he and Pork-pie had agreed that they would present a united front and while he reported to the authorities, she would take Sophie to the local surgery, pretending that she was a visiting relative who had fallen into the canal the night before and therefore needed to be checked over for adverse effects. It was a ruse they desperately hoped would allow them to keep the child with them for a little longer. At least until they had got to the bottom of who she was and how she came to be floating in the river and frighteningly close to drowning.

As well as all of this, there was the bird to consider and, of course, the cat, which had made itself at home in the boat and showed no signs of going anywhere in the foreseeable future.

Nevertheless, cats are cats and have a mind and life of their own and were therefore notorious for coming and going unannounced and unnoticed. He would deal with things one at a time and right now his priority was to get this thing over and done with.

It was at this point in his reverie that he heard loud voices and even louder wailing coming from the room into which the two children had been ushered. He couldn't hear the words nor get the gist of what was happening but it was quite apparent that the children were in trouble. His instincts told him to protect the innocent, but realising there was nothing much he could do, he forced himself to stay where he was until, just a few minutes later, another officer appeared from the depths of the police station and invited him to follow. He was led into another interview room sufficiently distanced and sound proofed to prevent further interruption.

***

"Well," said the somewhat supercilious officer as he closed the notebook rather more energetically than was strictly necessary, "I think that's about all for now. You are quite sure that the child is safe and you don't mind looking after it, erm her, until we can find somewhere more permanent or, better still, where she belongs?"

"Of course I don't mind," Kevin answered abruptly before clearing his throat and declaring, "I mean we'd be delighted to keep her for a while. Our concern, as I already stated, is that someone must be missing her and she seems unwilling or unable to tell us where she's come from..." he paused, realising that he had already said all of this and the look on the officer's face suggested in any case that he was no longer listening. "Right, so I'm free to go now, am I?" he finished and when the officer nodded in consent, he stood up, took his jacket from the back of the uncomfortably hard chair and held out his hand. No responding hand was proffered and so he left feeling as though he were a criminal rather than an upstanding citizen who was trying to do the right thing in reporting his 'find'.

'Finders keepers' he muttered to himself as he made his way out through the small maze of corridors.

"Vat's just what I say," said an unkempt and malodorous character who was shambling along in front of him, "I told 'em I found it but those bastards fink I stole it!"

"Pardon?" replied Kevin before realising that the speaker was not actually speaking to him but was rather opining to whoever might happen to be listening. In any case, Kevin had enough on his mind and wasn't particularly interested in whatever this dishevelled person might have or have not found.

On his way out through the entrance foyer, he noticed three children whom he presumed had been the perpetrators of the loud cries and wailing he had witnessed earlier. The youngest, a girl, was sobbing quietly as she sat on the wooden bench between the two boys, swinging her legs that were too short to reach the floor. She looked up as Kevin passed by and he winked at her as he smiled in a brief attempt to cheer her up. She sniffed, wiped her nose on her sleeve and rewarded him with an attempted smile. Kevin left the premises feeling that he might have achieved at least something positive. What a miserable and troubling morning it had been. All he wanted to do now was to get back to his cosy boat, make some strong coffee and find out how Porkpie had got on at the doctor's surgery.

***

"Clean bill of health! Doctor said," she announced, always brief with words, "Didn't like the bruises on her back and legs but could have been caused when she fell in the water. No lasting damage thank goodness." And as an afterthought, "No questions asked about who she was or where she came from. They're always too busy for niceties in that place."

So, first obstacles surmounted, Porkpie and Kevin began to consider 'what next?'

"Clothes and food I suppose," announced Porkpie just as Kevin opened his mouth to suggest, "Food and clothes!"

"You take her shopping and I'll sort out a meal," said Kevin and, after a pause, "birdseed and cat food too... please!"

The little grey cat had made itself well and truly at home and was currently curled up on top of the dog cage, fast asleep. The bird seemed to be gaining strength by the hour. It had begun to preen its glossy feathers and had pecked half-heartedly at the bowl of seeds but it was standing upright and its bright, though wary, eye followed every movement of cat, man or child.

As Porkpie wrapped a warm scarf around Sophie's neck and pulled a woolly hat firmly over her ears, an extraordinary, surprising and unaccustomed sense of warmth and contentment washed gently over Kevin who found himself grinning and humming quietly to himself as he set about preparing a meal for his newfound 'family'. "Don't be long!" he called after the fast-disappearing shoppers.

Chapter 7

You wouldn't have recognised the clean and tidy room that Carol stood back and surveyed. It had taken her the whole weekend but she had cleared and cleaned, thrown out and put away, washed and scrubbed as though her life depended upon it. She supposed, in a way, that it had. You could hardly call the way she had got through the last eighteen months, living, more a case of existing in some sort of black prison of her own making. She couldn't tell you anything that had happened during that time; days, weeks, months had come and gone in a foggy swirl of sameness where emotions didn't exist and nor did needs or wants. She knew from the bagginess of her clothes that she hadn't eaten much during that time and her lack lustre hair was now tied in a straggling knot in the nape of her neck. How had it got like this?

Well, unless you have experienced a severe depressive period in your life (and I sincerely hope that you have not) you will find it hard to understand how someone can let go of everything that used to be important whilst they sink into a morass of nothingness. It mattered not how many times other people had tried to help, and in the early days there had been many kindnesses offered to her, but despite them all she had slowly sunk into a state of oblivion – she was not even suicidal; that would have taken thought and feelings but of those she had none.

The day it happened had been much like any other typical day in late October. It was cold but sunny and the autumn colours were magnificent. After the morning chores were completed, she had decided to take Alfie to the park. A little boy of four, he loved nothing more than testing his strength on the climbing frame and kicking his ball into the fallen leaves.

Alfie had been in her care for about six months while his mother was recovering from a traumatic situation involving her abusive boyfriend and her attempts to disassociate herself from his controlling antics. She knew that Alfie had an older sister who was being cared for by the maternal grandmother and he wasn't the first child Carol had fostered. She had a very good reputation as a short-term foster mum for children in similar circumstances. She really loved the little children and caring for them gave her an outlet for the love she would have poured into her own child had things worked out differently for her. Married too young and a subsequent pregnancy which ended disastrously for both her and the stillborn baby, she was left without a husband and with no hope of bearing another child. And so, she had devoted herself to caring for other people's children – until...

"Time to go home for tea Alfie!" Carol called and held out her arms wide for him to run into and receive the hug she longed to give his wriggling little body. She laughed delightedly as he flew across the grass. But he ran right past her yelling, "Mum!"

Carol spun round and called again, "Alfie!" but he kept on running, straight across the road and straight into the path of an oncoming car. There was absolutely nothing she could have done to stop him. There was absolutely nothing she could do to bring him back. There was absolutely nothing left to care about or to live for...

***

A tear trickled down Carol's tired face as she remembered but she brushed it away with the back of her hand. Something had changed in her; someone needed her and for the first time in far too long she took a deep breath and began to look forward instead of remaining stuck in the depths of despair.

Wendy Crispin would be here in an hour; there was just time for a shower before she arrived and maybe she would find those scissors and cut off the mess of unruly hair that wouldn't stay tied.

***

Wendy was more than a little concerned about asking Carol to take on another foster child. Her fears had not been allayed in the slightest, if anything they were decidedly heightened, when she first saw the state of Carol and her home. However, the system, as always, was thoroughly over stretched and it was imperative that a place be found for the 9-year-old who had recently come onto their books. Having known Carol for a long time; they had gone to school together and although not close friends, she had always liked the girl; she had managed to persuade Burly Bob that they should at least give the woman a chance to come good.

A week had been agreed but when she peered through the windows half way through the week, nothing much had changed and Wendy was afraid that Carol was about to let her down. Thus it was that when a smiling, fresh and welcoming woman opened the door at her first knock, Wendy suddenly recognised the girl she had known all those years ago at school.

The transformation of Carol was reflected in her home and a short time later, Wendy bade her farewell with promises to arrange for her to meet the prospective foster child as soon as was convenient.

Carol smiled as she closed the door, breathed a sigh of relief and relaxed properly for the first time in far too many months.

Wendy smiled as she made her way back to the office and breathed a sigh of relief as she released the tension that had plagued her for far too many days.

***

He grunted as the barmaid pressed her finger into his forearm but didn't raise his head.

"Ups-a-daisy," she said, not unkindly, "Time to go 'ome. We're closing in 'alf'n'our! So orf yer go."

He raised his head from his arms, rolled off the barstool, wobbled his way across the bar-room, almost falling as he put out a hand to steady himself with the back of a chair, and waved vaguely in the direction of the barmaid, "Tah rah," he said as he staggered out of the pub.

The fresh air hit him and he reeled as realisation came. He crossed the road and began unsteadily to make his way home. Home? It was hardly that was it! It hadn't been the warm and cosy place that he associated with home for a long time. Usually it was cold, unwelcoming and thoroughly uncomfortable. Nevertheless, he was astonished to see blue flashing lights, several police cars, an ambulance and lots of tapes cordoning off his own front garden.

Chapter 8

Beanie couldn't wait for her sister to come home! She was bursting to tell her the tasty snippet of news she had just discovered on the early evening news. She bustled about putting ready the tea things and hoped that Mary would hurry back from wherever she had been today. When she came to think about it, she couldn't imagine what had kept her sister out for so long. It wasn't the nicest of days for a walk or to go fishing or bird-watching or any of the other outdoor activities that were Mary's usual practices but she had remembered her sister's request about unusual news items earlier that day. She was bound to be interested in this latest gem! Beanie (Beatrice) hummed softly to herself and decided to throw together a batch of scones to entice her sister home.

***

Porkpie had to admit to herself that she was getting a bit old for all this running about. Sophie had insisted on trying on every dress in the shop; or so it seemed, until she settled on a simple pinafore, a pair of jeans, two t-shirts and a warm cardigan. Some socks and undies and a pair of pyjamas were added to the pile together with some slippers and a pair of sturdy boots. All in all, it came to a tidy sum which Porkpie could ill afford but she handed over her credit card and made a mental note to eat a little less for the next few weeks.

She assumed that there must be a home with more clothing somewhere not too far away and belonging to the girl and although she also had to admit that she had rather enjoyed the afternoon, it was probably best if Sophie was returned to whence she came in the not too distant future. Meanwhile, she and Kevin would do their best to care for her until the mystery was solved. On the other hand, she couldn't help thinking that it would all be so much more straightforward if the child was a little more forthcoming.

Several times Porkpie had questioned gently; which way was home (as they waited for the bus)? What would her mother say (about a particularly unsuitable dress)? Did she wear a school uniform and if so which colours (there were several schools in the neighbouring towns and all had different coloured summer dresses for girls)? And other simple comments and queries. But all to no avail; Sophie was stoically silent on the subject of her previous experiences and gave absolutely nothing away whilst she raced excitedly from shop to shop, clothes rail to clothes rain and chattered nonstop about anything and everything except that which Porkpie really wanted to know.

Eventually they arrived back at the boat where Kevin had just lit the little stove and an appetising smell emanated from the small oven. Soon all three were cosily munching on hot pasties as they were closely watched by the fed and contented cat and the wary bird.

"Is it a rook?" piped up Sophie and without waiting for an answer, "If it is a rook, perhaps it's missing its friends; they nest in the tops of trees and you can see their nests when the leaves fall off. Perhaps it fell out! They can be a nuisance to the farmers but sometimes they chase the pigeons away which the farmer likes 'cos the pigeons are worse than rooks. I like the rooks but I like jackdaws better 'cos they talk to you. I don't like magpies 'cos they steal shiny things and they eat little birds too." She stopped to draw breath and was about to carry on chattering when Kevin interrupted, "Eat your food Sophie or it will get cold," and, after a pause, "Actually it's a crow."

Sophie's mouth fell open and a small crumb escaped from her lip but she remained silent and looked at the bird with wide eyes while she took in this new piece of information. "A crow!" she whispered in wonderment and then quietly continued to eat her meal whilst gazing at the glossy black bird.

When the meal was done, Porkpie stood up and reached for her coat as she announced that she ought to go home before her sister started to worry about her prolonged absence. "I'll come back in the morning," she promised, "You'll be alright, won't you? There's a toothbrush and some paste in the bag. Make sure she washes properly and don't let her stay up too long." With that she was gone and for a moment or two Kevin wondered what next, but Sophie solved the issue for him by demanding that he tell her about crows and other birds. He reached down a big book from the shelf above his head and before long the two of them were engrossed in the pictures and information it contained.

It was indeed rather later than he had intended when, at last, Sophie was curled up asleep in his sleeping bag on the sofa and Kevin resigned himself to a second, rather uncomfortable night on the floor. Tomorrow he would sort out the bedroom...

***

The figure crouching behind the hedge was invisible to anyone passing down the tow-path. Squashy hat pulled low and a scarf wound high over mouth and nose, no one would recognise the watcher even if they did happen to notice the shadowy shape as it silently followed Porkpie making her way home.

***

It must have been almost the middle of the night when Winnie awoke and realised that her big, brave brother was crying. "Billie!" she whispered as she slipped out of her bed and crossed the room to stand beside his. "Billie," more urgently, "Why are you crying? It's me what does that!"

Billie sniffed loudly and sat up, "You wouldn't understand," he began but as her lip dropped and the familiar miserable expression crossed her face, he lifted the edge of his duvet, "Come on in," he said, "you'll get cold out there. I'm alright really. I was just thinking about that horrible thing Frankie saw this morning. I'm glad we didn't go in. We're in enough trouble for going to steal cookies from her kitchen anyway. At least we're only grounded for a couple of days. Poor Frankie got it much worse than we did." He was going to say more but Winnie's tousled head nestled into his neck and her gentle breathing told him she was asleep. Most of the time his little sister was a pain in the backside, but at times like this she wasn't so bad after all.

***

"Where on earth have you been?" the unusually sharp greeting informed Porkpie of her sister's worried concern as to her lengthy absence.

"Sorry Bea," she replied, "lost track of time," and, in an attempt to appease Beanie's annoyance, "What's that delicious smell?"

In just a few minutes time, Beanie produced a plateful of scones, liberally buttered and with jam and cream on the side. Porkpie gingerly helped herself to two and slowly applied the toppings.

Beanie's scones were always delicious but Porkpie was already rather full of pasty. Oh well, she thought, I can always go without tomorrow. She smiled at her sister and remarked on how tasty the suppertime treat was but, "Never mind that!" Beanie retorted, bursting with the importance of her discovery, "Have you heard the news?"

"What news?" Porkpie was bemused by her unusually animated sister's abruptness, "Well no, obviously I haven't so go on, tell me," she encouraged.

"You'd never guess," Beanie was determined to make an impact with her impressive piece of information,

"No, I probably wouldn't," as Porkpie wondered to herself whether it had anything to do with Sophie. However, she couldn't have been more astonished when Beanie dramatically announced, "There's been a murder in our town!"

Chapter 9

It hadn't always been so miserable. In the early days, the dim and distant past, they had seemed to be idyllically happy and couldn't keep their hands off each other. How long ago had that been now? They had met soon after her husband had died in an accident at work. Construction was always a risky business and Wilfred much preferred to keep his feet firmly on the ground. He wasn't going to take the chance of falling from a great height onto some sharp implement or other. Her two children had grown up and flown the nest years before; both married with families of their own. Robert was halfway round the world and long established in New Zealand and Julie… well that was a sorry business and probably accounted for the downturn in all their lives.

Why she'd left that nice young man she married, he'd never understand and as for that other rapscallion she'd fallen in with, well, he'd never see what it was she saw in him! But then, it was none of his business who she chose to live with – she wasn't his daughter after all. And then the tragedy; tragic it was of course, but to take her own life and leave the little one to the mercies of – him (he couldn't even bear to think his name, let alone say it aloud) no wonder he'd turned to solace in a bottle. The only merciful blessing for the girl was her coming to live with her grandma and yet even that had become a double-edged benefit. He sighed and considered himself fortunate that he had no children of his own. More trouble than they're worth, he thought.

Gradually Wilfred opened his eyes and took in the unfamiliar room in which he'd spent the night. It wasn't much more than a glorified prison cell – and he'd seen the inside of a few of those in his time – however, they had assured him it was a hostel room, that it wasn't compulsory but that, if he wished, he could stay there whilst they sorted out the goings on in his own home.

It wasn't really his home; the house belonged to his wife, left to her by her parents, and she'd lived in it alone while he was languishing at her majesty's pleasure in one prison cell after another. He supposed she'd become used to being alone by the time he was eventually released. She hadn't seemed particularly pleased to see him when he knocked tentatively on her door. She hadn't welcomed him back into her bed or even her bedroom, but at least he had a room to himself, food on the table and enough cash to escape to the pub when her nagging became too much.

In any case, she hadn't much time for him, what with the two jobs she held down and looking out for that sniffling, skinny brat of a grand-daughter who was always poking her nose in where it had no business being poked. He wondered why he had ever thought it would have been a good thing for her to come and live with them. He already knew that she would have proved to be nothing but trouble with a capital T, just like her mother had been.

With a start, as he suddenly remembered the incident from the day before - the reason why he was in this room and not at home. He realised that it was somewhat unlikely that the girl would be going to live in that house after all! He supposed that he did feel a bit sad at the woman's horrible demise, she had been good to him even when he hadn't really deserved her kindness. Everything would be different now although not necessarily better. He remembered a one-time conversation about making wills and so he supposed the house would become his but he had no income with which to support it or even feed himself.

He wondered whether he could claim benefits or perhaps he'd have to sell the house and find somewhere cheaper to rent. As for the girl – well nothing had been said about her and there had been no sign of her during all the furore yesterday evening so, she'd run off, had she? Good riddance and one less problem to solve, he thought to himself as he pulled on his shabby, filthy clothes from the day before. He certainly wasn't going to mention her if no one else did. He closed the door behind him, turned the key before shoving it deep into his jacket pocket, and wandered towards the hostel cafeteria, wondering whom he could persuade to buy him a drink or two for his breakfast.

***

Beanie's interest in the local murder was short-lived. She was nothing if not disappointed by her sister's apparent lack of interest and she couldn't understand why Mary had developed a sudden interest in the marina. She watched the porkpie hat bobbing down the towpath in the direction of the moorings, for as far as she could see it behind the hedges. Although Mary had always been an outdoors sort of woman, she was far more likely to make her way downstream to the mill-race where she could watch the kingfishers feeding on the damsel flies, or across the little bridge to the waterside meadows where the spring flowers were beginning to show their colours. It really was most unusual for her to head for the boats and people.

In contrast, Porkpie couldn't wait to get to the boat and tell Kevin what her sister had told her. A murder in the small town of Potterton was extraordinary. It was one of those places where everyone knew everyone else's business; the comings and goings, the relationships both new and old, the births and deaths and despite her general disinterest in such gossip, Porkpie had kept her ear to the ground in case of news about a missing child. Somehow her instincts told her that there was some link, however tenuous, between the child's appearance in the river and the woman found dead on her kitchen floor.

Kevin was inclined to disagree and abruptly dismissed her tentative suggestion. He had promised to complete a repair job on one of the hire boats that was due to be taken out next weekend. Much as he would have liked to stay at home with Porkpie and Sophie, he needed the pay and to retain his reputation for efficiency and promptness. In a week's time it would be the Easter holidays and the hire business would be in full swing. There was always damage to one or other of the boats to be quickly seen to as well as maintaining the moorings and walkways used to access both owned and hired vessels.

He had wondered idly about finding where Sophie was schooled but the child was not forthcoming with any personal information and realising that there were very few school days left before the end of term, he decided to leave the subject for now in the hopes that Sophie would be more informative as she felt less threatened by the current situation. Despite her talkative and inquisitive nature, she was guarded and wary of divulging anything beyond the immediate.

***

Carol waited nervously on the park bench. Despite the warm spring sunshine, she shivered and pulled her coat more closely round her thin body. Today she was to meet the child. It had been a long time since she had been able to meet anyone, let alone leave the house, but she had promised Wendy that she would not let her down. So here she was.

They were late and she had just begun to think of going home to telephone and find out what had happened, when Wendy appeared at the park gates. Holding her hand and walking solemnly beside her was a small fair-haired girl. "Hi Carol, I'm so sorry we're a bit late. Tilda's bus was held up. I was worried that you might have thought we weren't coming."

"No – well yes actually," laughed Carol, her voice shaking with relief, "I did wonder what had happened but I'm glad you're here now." She bent down to look into Tilda's eyes and shook her small hand, "It's very nice to meet you at last," she said warmly. Tilda's smile lit up her face as she breathed, "Hello Aunty Carol."

"Aunty!?" Carol looked questioningly at Wendy, "I like that! Thank you." She said, grateful for the thoughtful gesture from the older woman.

"We thought it would be nicer for you and simpler and easier for Tilda to understand that her stay with you is temporary. A visit to an aunty is easy to explain to anyone who might wonder where she had been. She was worrying about telling her school friends why her mummy wasn't taking her to school. Not that we need worry about that for a couple of weeks anyway." Tilda had skipped across the playground to the swings and roundabout, leaving the two women free to discuss the details of Tilda's proposed stay.

The situation was straightforward; Tilda was not an endangered child, neither physically nor mentally abused, she had come into the care system on a temporary basis since her mother, a single parent, needed long term hospital treatment. There was no other family member to care for the little girl whilst her mother was incapacitated and so, when Wendy heard of her plight, she remembered Carol's sad story and began to realise that there may here be an opportunity for two people in need to help each other out. As she watched the little girl and the middle-aged woman laughing quietly together as they played on the park equipment, she hoped very much that her instincts had proved sound.

Friday – that would be the day everything could change for Carol. It was difficult to imagine looking after another child after the tragedy of Alfie but there were enough differences; age, gender, reasons and personality, to make it easier to avoid making comparisons. Most importantly, Tilda would know where her mother was and she was sufficiently sensible not to run across a busy road without looking.

After Wendy and Tilda had left, Carol found herself looking forward to Friday. At long last she once more felt she had a purpose and a reason to move on with her life. She hoped very much that Tilda would enjoy her stay.

Chapter 10

Frankie was king of the playground on Monday morning. Billie and Winnie stood to one side and watched whilst Frankie elaborated on their 'find'. All the other children listened wide-eyed and wide-mouthed as he described, with a lot of extra detail, most of which he had taken straight from a television programme, how he had found the woman's body lying in a pool of her own blood.

"Beside her was a knife and an 'ammer, all covered in blood," he explained, pausing dramatically for effect.

"How did you know she was dead?" asked a small boy.

"Put me fingers on her wrist didn' I!" Frankie, untruthfully, declared, and went on, "anyways she was stone cold and smelled something awful. She must 'ave been there for ages."

"Why did you go there in the first place?" a much more relevant question from one of the older boys. For a moment Frankie was stumped; he couldn't exactly admit that he was intending to steal from her kitchen – that would lead to too big a loss of kudos.

"We was just passing," he began, "the door was open and…" but he was saved from further invention by the arrival of Mrs Wells who had been summoned by a perplexed caretaker wondering what on earth the children were doing still in the playground long after the morning bell had been rung.

St Cecelia Primary School catered for most of the village children as well as serving the population of the small town of Potterton. It wasn't a large school with just under one hundred pupils but with almost half of those children coming from the outer areas, it served as a meeting point for many different families. Mrs Wells was a popular Head Teacher and on that particular morning she had been waylaid by the arrival of Wendy Crispin who had come to arrange for Tilda to attend St Cecelia's whilst she was in the care of Carol Porter. Had she noticed the pow-wow taking place in the playground, she would have nipped it in the bud before young Frankie could elucidate on his experience of the gruesome find.

She sighed as she ushered all of the children into the assembly hall and realised that some of the younger pupils were obviously distressed and disturbed by Frankie's pronouncements. So much for her well-prepared assembly plans; she had spent half the weekend working on a cross-school presentation on Easter and its meanings both religious and secular. Now she must work off the cuff and talk to these children about interfering in things that should not concern them.

She would need to talk sternly to young Frankie. He was old enough to know better than to frighten the little ones with gory tales, and the pale and drawn faces of Billie and Winnie Frost had not gone unnoticed. Perhaps she should talk to them too. Still, it was the variety of circumstances and the differing needs of the children in her care that had kept her at the helm of this school for more than eighteen years, she was confident that, together with her team of experienced teachers, she could ride this storm and come out smiling when the gathering clouds had dispersed.

By the end of her assembly it was time for morning break and she sent the children outside; the older ones to the games area and the little ones onto the playground. Frankie, Billie and Winnie sat disconsolately on a row of chairs outside Mrs Wells' office door. Winnie was sniffling as usual and kindly Miss Humphries, the secretary, handed her a tissue and told her to blow her nose.

Mrs Wells was on the telephone to the local constabulary; she wanted to be sure of any details before she confronted Frankie.

"I see, thank you," they heard her say as Miss Humphries opened the door and disappeared inside. A moment later the door opened again and Mrs Wells invited the three youngsters into her room. They stood, hands behind their backs, heads bowed, in an expectant row. No one was invited into Mrs Wells' room unless they had been bad or very good; none of the three believed they were there to be praised.

Winnie continued to sniff and Mrs Wells addressed her first, "Come closer," she said, holding out her hand to the little girl, "I think you've had a nasty shock and maybe seen something unpleasant," but Winnie shook her head violently, setting her curls swinging, "I never saw nuffink!" she declared.

"Well, that's a good thing then, isn't it?" Mrs Wells spoke softly, "So there's nothing to be upset about is there? You haven't done anything wrong; you were just in the wrong place at a bad time. Now, dry your eyes, blow your nose and run back to your classroom. Try not to think about all this nasty business and it will soon be all sorted out so you can forget all about it."

Once Winnie had gone, Mrs Wells turned her attention to Billie. "What about you, young man?" she began and he immediately avowed, "I never saw nuffink either; it was Fran…" Mrs Wells held up her hand, "Enough," she stopped him, "and it's 'nothing'. Better still, you didn't see anything," she corrected. Billie's head drooped at the admonishment and he shook with the injustice of being pulled up for something that Winnie had got away with. However, he soon forgot his woes as Mrs Wells asked him to explain exactly why they were at the house in Meadow Walk. His first instinct was to lie again and say that they were just passing but something made him realise that he'd be better telling the truth. It was bad enough of them to have intended stealing from the lady's kitchen, but nothing could have prepared either of them for what they ultimately witnessed.

"We were going to take some cookies, 'cos she bakes really nice ones," he stopped, realising that she wouldn't be baking any more cookies now, "I mean she used to…" he stuttered and sniffed hard. "Frankie went to see if the coast was clear, I mean to see if anyone was in the kitchen," he explained, "when he came running out, looking scared…"

"I weren't scared." Frankie's bravado was wearing thin but Mrs Wells' hand stopped him again, "You'll have your turn when I've heard Billie out," she explained, "Go on Billie."

"When he came running out, I peeked through the door but all I could see was a pair of legs and some pink slippers. I didn't see no blood or nuffing but I didn't stop to look for anyfing else."

"Thank you," Mrs Wells smiled at Billie and he relaxed. "What did you do next?" she asked.

"Well, we talked for a bit and then Frankie went to his friend's house and Winnie and I went to the police to tell them about the lady. They called Mum and she came and brought Frankie and his mum too. We told them everyfink I've told you."

"Just one more question," she said, "Did you know the lady who lived in that house?"

"No," he hesitated to admit, "but we've been there before – to get cookies," he explained.

Frankie's version of events mirrored Billie's with the added detail of his actually seeing the woman's body and realising she was dead. It was while he was describing that part to Mrs Wells that his spirit suddenly broke and he cried noisily and copiously while she comforted and reassured him that he wasn't in any trouble; that his description could be very helpful to the police and that the only part about which she was cross with him was the way he had told all the other children. "You must understand that some of those little children might be very frightened by what you told them. You saw how upset Winnie was but you didn't stop to think that some of the others might also have been distressed by what you described."

"I know," Frankie mumbled, "I'm sorry, but Winnie is always crying," he began to make excuses but Mrs Wells halted him once more saying, "that's no excuse, Frankie, she might be inclined to cry but this really was something to be upset about, don't you think?"

"Yeah… I s'pose… Sorry," he hiccoughed.

"I think perhaps you might have been a little bit frightened yourself," she gently suggested and the fresh onslaught of tears confirmed her suspicions. She let him cry noisily for a few minutes before handing him some tissues and saying briskly, "Right, go and tidy yourself up. Wash your face in the cloakroom and go back to your class. You've got learning to do today – more than you've already done so far!" She smiled at him and he gave her a watery grin in return. Just as he reached the door, he turned and said, "One more fing, you asked Billie if he knew the lady who die…"

"Yes?"

"Well, I don't – didn't know her but there's a girl who comes to this school who is sometimes there. I think that's who she bakes – baked the cookies for."

Chapter 11

Although it was quite normal for them not to see eye to eye, it was extremely abnormal for them to argue quite so vociferously.

"I just don't think it's right!" she declared, "What will people think?"

"Since when have I been concerned with what people think?" came the retorted reply, "if you're worried on your own account then stay out of other people's business and stop following me around. If you hadn't been so nosey you wouldn't have known anything to get in such a stew and be so worried about!"

"But it's just not done; a young girl staying on a boat with an older man. People will come up with all sorts of reasons why it shouldn't be allowed." Beanie was tired of trying to make her sister see sense and Porkpie was more than a little annoyed by her interfering sister's opinions.

Sophie was happy, Kevin, with her help, was coping very well with the demands of the young girl and no one, other than Beatrice, appeared to be unhappy with the situation.

"Well, if you aren't going to do anything about it, I might have to take things into my own hands." Beanie was not going to let it go lightly. This latest threat incensed her sister to such an extent that she stood up abruptly, over-turning a small side table as she did so, declaring, "If you do any such thing, I'll never speak to you again." Thoroughly upset, she flounced out of the house, slamming the door behind her, and strode off down the path towards Kevin's boat without so much as a glance to left or right.

Had she done differently, she might have noticed the squashy hat as it swiftly disappeared below the top of the hedge that surrounded the small cabin.

***

Porkpie was greeted warmly by the little grey cat winding itself in and out of her legs and purring loudly. She tapped lightly on the roof of the boat and without waiting for a response, stepped down into the well. Before opening the door, she paused for a moment and took a deep breath. In her heart she knew that her sister was right about the impropriety of a young girl staying with a single, unrelated man but she very much resented Beanie's interference and she had been somewhat sneaky in her investigations of Porkpie's current unusual behaviours. She would talk to Kevin about the situation and together they would come up with a plan.

She smiled to herself at the thought of them sharing the care of this child. Although love and marriage had never really been on her list of desires for herself, she had to admit that there were times when the thought of someone with whom to share life's joys and iniquities had briefly crossed her mind. Then she laughed at herself; Kevin was half her age and a confirmed bachelor; a hermit almost, of course he wouldn't be romantically interested in someone like her.

Equilibrium restored, she pushed open the door and was immediately struck by how silent everything was. No chattering or laughing from either child or bird, no music playing and no evidence of anyone other than the boat's usual occupant who would, of course, be out working at this time of day. So where was Sophie? They had established a simple routine where Kevin would give Sophie her breakfast and then set off for work knowing that Porkpie would arrive to spend time with the girl until he could return whenever his tasks for the day were done. It suited them all; Sophie was pleased to be trusted with a degree of independence, Kevin was able to work uninterrupted and Porkpie was happy to help out for the time being. Obviously, this couldn't go on for ever. It was important to discover where Sophie really belonged or to make more permanent arrangements for her long-term future. But, for the time being, the system worked well except…

Where could she be? Porkpie quickly investigated the very small area of the cabin, the smaller bedroom and the little foredeck but there was no sign of the girl. Even the crow was silent in the cage which was covered over with a blanket. Was it still in there? Porkpie lifted a corner of the cover and was astonished to see both the bird and the girl curled up inside the cage and fast asleep! Silently she dropped the curtain back down and quietly made herself a pot of tea, fed the cat and began to read the book she'd brought with her. However, she'd barely read half a page when there was a knock on the cabin roof.

As she arose to see who was there, she was halted by a whispered, "Don't!"

"Don't what?"

"Don't let them in," Sophie sounded scared and agitated.

"Doesn't that depend on who it is?" Porkpie spoke softly.

"I know who it is," a sob broke from Sophie's hidden body, "They've come to take me away and I don't want to go anywhere else." By this time, the knocking had become sharper and more insistent and a voice called, "I know you're in there; I can hear you whispering!"

Porkpie wanted to ask Sophie who would want to take her away and where they would take her but the urgency of the knocking made her put her questions aside. "Stay silent," she commanded, "and I'll see who it is and what they want."

"Who were you talking to?" the sharp question came even before the door was fully opened and the burly man who filled the small cockpit-well tried to peer around Porkpie's slight frame.

"No one," she replied, "I was talking to myself; I do that a lot," she explained but the man wasn't so easily dissuaded. He continued to try to see round her but, despite the smallness of her body, she was tall enough to need to bend her head to get through the narrow door and he was obliged to step back before she head butted him in his overlarge paunch as she came out into the well. She closed the door behind her saying in explanation, "keeping the warmth inside and the cold out". "How can I help you, sir?" she enquired more solicitously than was necessary, thus disarming his belligerent opening.

It transpired that he had been sent from Social Services. Porkpie's immediate reaction was one of absolute fury directed at her interfering sister. However, almost as quickly it occurred to her that, despite her threat, it couldn't have been Beanie who had summonsed social services. There was no way that someone would have been dispatched to investigate that quickly. Perhaps she owed her sister an apology…

Big Bob's mission, in response to Kevin's report to the police concerning a child he had found, was to ensure that the child was being properly cared for whilst they continued their investigation as to where she might have come from. Porkpie was pleased to ascertain that there were still no reports of a missing child and to assure the man that Sophie was being well looked after, "She's in school of course," she lied, but kept her fingers crossed behind her back whilst hoping that he wouldn't ask which school. Fortunately, he did not, which may well have been because there was only one school in the area and so it wasn't unreasonable to assume that she too attended there.

Just as he was finishing making a few notes on the pad attached to his clip-board, a loud squawk came from within the cabin followed by a slightly less loud 'shhh',

"What was that?" he asked sharply and looking accusingly at her, "I thought you said you were alone in there?"

"I was, I mean I am," Porkpie was momentarily flustered, "it's the bird," she explained. Bob looked at her curiously, "A bird, eh?"

"Yes, a bird," she went on to explain that it was a wild bird and was recovering from an accident. "It's very intelligent and is an excellent mimic. It's really important to keep it quiet and undisturbed," she gabbled, "I'll have to go and settle it now. Goodbye and thanks for coming." She almost pushed him out of the boat and across the narrow gang-plank onto the slippery bank. He stumbled across, almost falling back into the water, and dropped his clip-board into the mud.

Porkpie didn't know whether to laugh or cry. She had never felt so flustered in her life before. Usually, she was stoic, self-assured and controlled but today she felt neither. She had argued with her sister, she had just lied to someone in authority and had almost assaulted the man, but her sense of the ridiculous bubbled up in merriment which she only just managed to contain until he was safely out of earshot and she was back inside the cabin.

"Aunty Pie, what is so funny?" asked the puzzled little girl but the fun was infectious and before long they were both crying with laughter without really knowing what had caused their mirth. Even the bird flapped and squawked with them.

Big Bob was rarely put out by people's idiosyncrasies but there was something odd about the conversation he had just had. Wendy, his boss, had mentioned a lady who was sharing the care of the foundling, but she had failed to note just how oddly that particular lady behaved. "Ah well, people!" he breathed to himself as he rubbed ineffectually at the now thoroughly muddied and almost illegible notes he had made. "Just as well I'm not too bothered about the girl, although I haven't actually seen her yet," he mused and then dismissed the morning's events as he moved on to his next case.

Chapter 12

Wilfred sat hunched over a paper cup of by now tepid coffee. In his opinion, he had been kept waiting far too long. He'd come here of his own volition and at their invitation; it was rude of them to keep him waiting in the dull, windowless room. It did, however, give him time to mull over his current situation. Firstly, he needed to go home to get some clean clothes and, secondly, he wanted some answers to the questions that had been plaguing him ever since he had woken in that impersonal hostel room. Thirdly, he really needed another drink; something a bit stronger than cold coffee.

His memory of the recent past was vague to put it mildly. He and Milly had argued mightily. That wasn't unusual in itself but this time she had packed his things in a carrier bag and thrown them out into the front garden, with instructions for him not to come back until he was properly sober. He remembered leaving the house and he remembered catching a bus to the city. He didn't remember having any idea of where he was actually going or what he was intending to do. Whatever it was, he didn't do it. He had entered the first public house he came to as he wandered the city streets and before very long was more or less catatonically comatose, a state with which he was generally familiar and in which there was no need to think, care or feel anything at all. He had no idea of the time, day or even month as had been a more or less permanent state of affairs for the last two years.

DI Evans, shook his head as he thought to himself that it was no wonder that the woman had chucked him out. What a pitiful specimen and drunken waste of space he appeared to be. However, and on the other hand, it seemed extremely unlikely that his particular apology of a man could have murdered his wife and there appeared to be no evidence to suggest foul play. He made a note of the bus journey into the city and although Wilfred had no idea of the name of the pub he had entered, he knew that it was within reasonable walking distance of the bus station and was therefore likely to be fairly close by. He would send some of his team to check out the local hostelries to confirm the man's alibi. Having no good reason to detain him any longer, he dismissed him with a caution and an order not to leave the town until the case was resolved.

After a stiff drink at the Pig and Whistle, Wilfred made his way home. On reaching the front door, he fumbled in his pockets for a key. He tried the key he found in his jacket pocket and then remembered that it was the key to a hostel room. He swore softly to himself before making his way down the side of the house, remembering that the last time he'd been at home he'd flung open the back door before leaving through the front. The door was locked. What was he to do? He badly needed a bath and some clean clothes and to sleep in his own bed. He scratched his head and muttered to himself, "What the bloody hell am I supposed to do now?"

"Cooey!" at first, he ignored the call. The last thing he needed was a nosey neighbour asking questions. He closed his eyes and leant his head against the door, "I really need a drink," he surmised.

Two minutes later, he almost jumped out of his skin when a hand tapped him on the shoulder. "What the blazes…" he began but before he could continue, the round face of his wife's friend, Sharon, came into focus and he realised she was talking to him, "… so here I am and here it is." She held out a cardboard box on the top of which was a keyring and two keys. "She asked me to look after them when she locked herself out not so long ago. I thought you might need them. And I brought your bag of things back too. You left it on the front lawn the other day."

Wilfred shook his head, peered at the woman's kindly, smiling face, and took the bag and the proffered keys. He fumbled at the lock for a moment or two before successfully opening the door and stepping inside.

He hadn't been sure what to expect. The last time he'd looked into this kitchen it had been a very different picture. He vaguely remembered seeing Milly lying on the floor and an overturned stool half on top of her. He remembered broken glass and a large quantity of blood in which Milly's hair was

72

spread and gradually turning pink. He hadn't stopped to take in any further details. Still sufficiently inebriated from the days before, he had simply turned away and gone to the Pig and Whistle to drown out any thought or speculation about the truth of the matter.

"Shall I put it in the fridge for you?" Sharon had entered the kitchen behind him and was also looking at the clean and tidy room. There was no evidence at all of the recent horrific event; all was scrubbed clean and everything in its place. The only item out of the ordinary was a cooling rack on the kitchen table on which were the cookies that had so tempted the small boys we met previously.

Absent-mindedly, Wilfred picked up one of the biscuits and bit into it. Having been left out in the air for several days, it was soft and chewy, not crisp and fresh as he had expected. He ate the rest of that one but picked up the tray and tipped its contents into the waste bin. In order to do so, he was obliged to walk around the woman standing in his kitchen and holding a cardboard box.

"In the fridge?" she repeated.

"What? Oh! Yeah, thanks," he managed to stutter before sitting down abruptly on a kitchen chair and putting his head on his arms as they lay folded on the table.

"Are you sure you're going to be alright?" enquired the kindly neighbour, "I can come back in a while if you need anything else, but I need to go and see to the cat at number 14 next. It's just had kittens," she explained. "Well not just, they're about old enough to go to new homes now but the Smiths are away until next week so I'm feeding them all…" She prattled on but he wasn't really listening and so it was with some surprise, when he eventually lifted his head, that he observed she was gone.

What was it the DI had said? Something about not leaving town? Something about not suspecting foul play? Wilfred was quite sure he hadn't said anything about not drinking so having hauled himself to his feet and up the stairs, he bathed and changed his clothes (which he had to retrieve from the carrier bag that Sharon had handed to him outside), he closed and locked the back door from the inside and left the house via the front door and, as usual, having placed the key under the mat, made his way to the nearest pub for his liquid supper.

Much to his amazement, he was met with solicitous kindness by the barmaid who led him to his usual barstool and handed him his favourite tipple. "We all 'eard what 'appened to your wife. Such a sorry situation. I'm glad to see you back 'ere again. No one knew where you'd gorn. Are you alright?"

Wilfred didn't know how to answer that question. He didn't really know what 'alright' was any more other than being in a pub with a drink in his hand so he simply nodded and attempted to smile.

"If you need anything else, just ask," she said and went back behind the bar to serve other waiting customers.

A little later, she tapped him on the shoulder and suggested it might be time for him to go home. Unusually he was ready to do so. All he had heard were whispered conversations which seemed to suggest that he was in some way to blame for his wife's misfortune. He'd tried to ignore them all but something was nagging at the back of his mind; something concerning a child. For so long he had put aside all thoughts of anyone else but, despite the alcoholic fog that clouded his brain, this particular niggle would not leave him alone. Accordingly, he thanked the barmaid, pulled on his jacket and, a little less unsteadily than on previous occasions, made his way home.

The key was under the mat as he had left it and a plateful of the shepherd's pie Sharon had placed in his fridge was soon heated in the microwave and gratefully eaten. Wilfred suddenly felt more comfortable and alive than he had for a very long time.

Chapter 13

It was the first Wednesday after the Easter break and Beanie was looking forward to the Sip and Stitch meeting that afternoon. Whilst they took a break during the school holidays she had missed the gossip and interesting snippets of information that she managed to glean from the other ladies in the group. She'd tried a book club, but found it too hard to keep up with the rather erudite and in-depth discussions of the peculiar novels the organisers chose, and she'd joined the church choir for a short while.

Everyone was terribly intense at those rehearsals and since she couldn't make head nor tail of the lines and dots on the music they were expected to read and sing, she decided that particular activity was not for her either. Bell ringing was far too strenuous and the walking group went on such long, circuitous routes that she had no breath for talking to anyone. No, it transpired that Sip and Stitch was by far the best option for her. It left her free to read whatever took her fancy, to hum along to Songs of Praise with no one scowling at her inaccuracies and to walk as much or as little as she chose.

She wasn't really a knitter but the group had decided to make blankets for charity and so she had volunteered to sew together, into rugs and throws of various sizes, all the squares they produced. It had turned out to be a much larger task than she had anticipated since they were all quite prolific knitters but she was pleased with the work she had produced and was anxious to pass her handiwork on to the group organisers. Above all, she was looking forward to the gossip and a chance to tell the other ladies all about the excitement she had experienced during the past few weeks; a girl in the water, an argument with her sister, the little grey cat that followed Porkpie about and the mysterious figure with a squashy hat that she kept seeing in odd places.

Despite the fact that all the attendees seemed to have a lot to say for themselves, Beanie was quite satisfied with the outcome of her contributions to the conversations and everyone was very complimentary about the blankets she'd finished. There were plenty of oohs and ahs and even one or two gasps when she told them about the girl in the river who had survived in spite of her nearly drowning. Most of the ladies were as appalled as she had been at the idea of the little girl staying aboard his boat with a single man and there were plenty of tuts and shaken heads when she mentioned the argument with her sister.

Beanie began to feel quite vindicated in her opinion that it just wasn't 'right'. The most satisfying bit of gossip that she managed to glean was concerning the little cat. Sharon, who had almost stolen Beanie's thunder with her tale of the possible murder of her friend and neighbour, had, in passing, mentioned a cat and some kittens that she was caring for whilst another neighbour was away from home. She happened to say that she had expected to be caring for four little kits but that there were actually only three. "Perhaps my friend had counted the queen as well," she surmised.

Beanie, remembering that her sister had mentioned a cat, decided not to follow up the idea during the meeting but she would most certainly mention it to Porkpie when she got home.

No one had seemed particularly interested in the man with the squashy hat but as she was making her way home later that afternoon, and as she rounded a bend in the towpath, Beanie was almost certain that she saw the man stepping off Kevin's boat. It was the hat that took her attention; it was quite distinctive in an understated sort of way; khaki, wide brimmed but ill-fitting and floppy, it was inclined to bob up and down as the wearer walked or, on this occasion, almost ran, although awkwardly as if carrying a heavy load, down the path and away from where Beanie was approaching her home.

Shaking her head, she admonished herself for an over active imagination, "it was probably just Kevin in a hurry to be somewhere," she muttered to herself as she turned in through the garden gate and admired the primroses that lined the path while making her way to her own front door.

***

"She's gone!" All thoughts of talking to Kevin about schools, uniforms or any other subject that had hitherto seemed important, had disappeared just as soon as Porkpie realised that Sophie was nowhere to be found.

"She can't be," Kevin was rather more prosaic in not believing the enormity of what she was saying.

"But she is," with a sob, Porkpie repeated, "She's gone. I've looked everywhere."

Kevin hurried down the length of his floating home, checked the foredeck and the cage where the bird stood with its head cocked on one side as if to say, 'told you so', and then he made his way to the newly tidied and properly made bedroom where the only living thing was the cat curled up asleep on the pillow. The washroom door was open and the small galley similarly deserted. Reluctantly he was obliged to acknowledge that his friend was right; Sophie was not aboard the boat.

"Could she have just gone for a walk?" he didn't really believe that idea himself. So far Sophie had made no attempt to go anywhere on her own. Indeed, she had seemed almost reluctant to be anywhere other than inside the cosy cabin. Porkpie shook her head, "I've looked in both directions," she assured him and indicated the telescope she'd left on the work surface, evidencing the diligence with which she had looked.

"Maybe she left a note?" Kevin was by now clutching at straws.

"I've looked for one of those too," Porkpie was telling the truth. It had been about twenty minutes since she'd got back from the store where she had gone to buy milk and eggs to make supper. "Sophie was playing with the cat and promised to stay where she was until I got back. I was only gone for about twelve minutes." Porkpie was beside herself with worry and upset. Where could the child be. With a sudden gasp of realisation, Porkpie cried, "In the river? Again?" They both hurried out of the boat, Kevin clutching a boat-hook and Porkpie a towel but there was no sign of any disturbance to the bank or the water. Everything was quiet and peaceful in the early evening spring air and a graceful swan glided slowly by. It nodded to the anxiously seeking pair as if to say, "Nothing out of the ordinary here."

"What to do now?" Kevin voiced what they were both thinking. They could go to the police but what to say? The child they had found was now lost again? They would begin to look like some sort of pair of half-crazed lunatics who liked causing a stir with stories of lost children. Even the social worker who had come in response to their initial statement had not actually seen the child and had not even followed up with a report of his visit since he had the distinct impression that the 'lady' involved was a bit cuckoo and there probably was no child. Perhaps she was some sort of demented childless spinster who liked imagining that her non-existent child was missing. In any case, there had been no reports of missing children; either locally or nationally, so there was definitely something a bit 'odd' about the whole affair.

Eventually and rather reluctantly, Porkpie decided she should go home to her sister. She would tell her everything; of all the people she had anything to do with (although, truth to tell, that didn't amount to very many), at least her sister would believe her and might even be able to suggest something helpful. Perhaps it would have been better if she had listened to Beanie's objections in the first place…

Chapter 14

Tilda was settling well with 'Aunty Carol' and at St Cecilia's School. Frankie, Billie and Winnie had been appeased with plenty of chocolate eggs, ice creams and visits to the zoo and soon forgot about the horrible thing they had witnessed.

Easter weekend seemed a long time ago although it was actually a little less than a week since the summer term began and only eight days since Sophie had disappeared. In the meantime, Kevin was rushed off his feet with work to be done by yesterday and Porkpie was trying her hardest to do as her sister suggested, and stop worrying and wondering about Sophie and what had happened to her.

Life seemed to be going on as normal, just as though nothing had changed. But everything had changed for Porkpie and, try as she might, she could not put Sophie out of her head. She just knew, without any hope of explaining it to anyone else, that something was terribly wrong and she simply could not sit back and accept the situation. There must be a way of finding out what had happened.

She thought of going to the police to ask what if anything they had discovered about the girl she and Kevin had 'found'. Since there were still no reports of missing children, they would be disinterested and dismissive of her concerns.

She thought of contacting Social Services to ask if anything had come of their investigations. They were kind and conciliatory but since she was no relation to the possibly missing child, there was nothing more they could do.

She puzzled and fretted and worried until Beanie became very concerned for her sister's mental welfare. It wasn't until after she had been to a subsequent weekly Sip and Stitch meeting that she was reminded of the story about a cat and kittens.

Sharon had been holding forth about the unfortunate death of her neighbour; "It transpired that there was no foul play and she hadn't been murdered at all. Although I must say that I thought it was that drunken husband of hers who had done the deed. It was clever of him to make it look as though she'd fallen off a kitchen stool. He even broke a vase, cut her wrist with it and scattered the glass around. I say he pulled stuff from the cupboards to make it look like an intruder had murdered her. He's a right bastard that one!"

Some of the older ladies, gasped at her choice language but one of the younger, bolder women suggested, "Perhaps she was spring cleaning her kitchen and fell? The newspaper report said that the husband hadn't been at home for several days."

"Harumph!" grunted Sharon, "an accident? My ar… foot!" she checked herself. Realising that she'd probably done the subject to death (if you'll pardon the pun), she moved swiftly on to the subject of the missing kitten. "I was right you know!" she stated with a satisfied smirk, realising she was on safer ground with this particular snippet, "There should have been four kittens. One was missing!"

There were a few tuts and gasps from the assembled company and then,

"What did the missing kitten look like?" Beanie softly enquired but shrank back at the disparaging glare Sharon threw in her direction. "How should I know? I didn't see it 'cos it wasn't there, remember?"

"Well, what did the others look like?" Beanie insisted in a mild but determined tone, "Perhaps they were all quite similar," she suggested.

There was a pause and a moment of anticipatory silence before, "Hmm, come to think of it, yes, they were all grey but with different patches of white here and there."

"Ah, thank you," breathed Beanie. Perhaps this was something she could mention to Mary, her sister, and give her something else to think about.

The conversation moved on to plans for future projects, holidays and other gossip, whilst Beanie considered how to approach the subject with her unusually touchy sister.

***

She was cold. It was dark in the windowless space, which didn't really qualify as a room, and she was hungry. She thought about calling out to see if someone could bring her a sandwich and some water but she remembered his final words as he closed and locked the door, "Keep quiet, Brat!"

Had she known the phrase, she would have said that she was experiencing déjà vu and although she could remember numerous times when her mother had shoved her into a cupboard to hide her firstly from her father and then, later, from Dave, this was definitely different. Always before, when she had heard the cruel words flung at her mother, she had recognised the fear in her mother's conciliatory responses and although she hadn't understood why or what from, she knew that her mother was in some way protecting her from Dave.

Dave had come into their lives soon after her baby brother had been born. Mum and Dad had argued a lot when Mum's belly began to swell. She remembered Mum pleading with Dad and Dad's angry refusal to have anything to do with the new baby's imminent arrival.

"I don't even know that it's mine!" he yelled at her and in reply, she sobbed, "Who else's do you think it could be?"

"Well now, that's a very good question," she could hear the scorn in her father's tone, "How many have there been? I know all about Phil of course…"

"You know nothing about Phil," her mother tearfully retorted but before she could say more there was a resounding slap of hand on cheek and Mum's body slumped down in front of the slatted door of the cupboard where she was hiding. Silently, she cried.

She didn't like to think about that horrible time when her young world had fallen apart. She never saw her father again, not even when the baby was born. But things began to get better once Granny Milly and Uncle Wilfred came to stay for a while.

After that, there were a few years when everything was good. Baby Alfie was a blessing to them all and Mum seemed happy in her new relationship with Dave. What she didn't see was the unkind way that Dave treated Sophie. He never called her by name; it was always some derogatory term such as 'Brat', 'Nuisance' or worse, and he expected her to fetch and carry for him as well as keeping out of his way when his 'friends' came to the house.

By the time Alfie was four years old, Sophie was at school and Mum had a part time job. Things were looking up and Mum could afford for Alfie to go to a child-minder during her working days. Sophie enjoyed school and the freedom it gave her to get away from Dave's unreasonable demands, although she often took her time about walking home at the end of the school day. She hated being in the house alone with that man and there was no way she was ever going to think of him as her father.

The final denouement had come when the tragic accident happened and little Alfie was taken from them. She hadn't really understood her mother's devastation, after all, she was still there to be loved and cared for, wasn't she? Perhaps Mum could make another baby; she was still young and pretty…

However, no swelling tummy evidenced another baby and nothing much changed at home except that Mum cried a lot and Dave's friends came round more and more often. Sophie began to despair of ever being happy at home again but then, about a year and half after Alfie had died, she overheard a conversation between her mother and Dave.

"That's it. I'm leaving. Right now."

"But what will I do without you? Who will help me to look after Sophie? I need you Dave," her mother pleaded with him to stay.

"What you need is to get your head sorted out!" Dave said coldly, "I'm tired of your tantrums and your tears, it's always about you. When do I get some sympathy?" and before she had managed to formulate an answer, "Perhaps you should have her fostered. That would give you time and space to get to grips with life."

Her horror at the suggestion of being fostered blotted out any further hearing of the conversation. There was no way she was going to live with a stranger. Maybe she could go and stay with Granny Milly…?

The following morning, she hadn't been surprised, in fact quite the opposite, when Dave was missing from the breakfast table, but she was very upset that her mum hadn't even set the table for the two of them. Sophie carefully prepared a tray for her mother with a mug of tea and a slice of buttered toast. She knocked on her mother's bedroom door but placed the tray on the floor outside it when there was no response from within. She didn't say 'goodbye' because she didn't want her mother to follow her.

Carefully she packed a small bag and helped herself to a few coins from Mum's purse. She would catch the bus to Potterton; she thought she could remember the way to Granny's house...

Chapter 15

"Beanie, you're a genius!" Porkpie beamed at her sister and for the first time in days she felt optimistic.

"Well Pie dear, I couldn't bear to watch you moping about the place and when I heard about the missing cat, I remembered what you'd told me about the little creature that appeared at the same time as the girl." The two sisters hugged each other and then stood back and smiled awkwardly, both acknowledging the unusually demonstrative action. "Off you go then dear. I'll bake us a nice cake for when you get back." Beanie bustled out into the kitchen and Porkpie took her coat from a hook by the door, put her purse in her pocket and set off for the address her sister had given her.

She stopped by Kevin's boat on her way through the marina, hoping she could tell him the good news, but he was not on board. It was such a busy time of year for him and she even felt a little jealous that he had so much to keep his mind occupied, unlike her who could think of little else except for Sophie's disappearance.

It wasn't until she reached the turning into Meadow Walk, that she realised she was in the same vicinity as the suspected murder victim. Of course, it had since transpired that there was no murder, but still she felt a tingle down her spine as she thought of the dead woman lying on her kitchen floor. She idly wondered which house it was but had no time to think further when she found herself outside number 9 which was where Beanie's friend, Sharon lived. She knocked tentatively and was rewarded with, "Coming. Hang on a jiffy," before Sharon's head appeared at an upstairs window.

"Oh hello, I'm Mary," she explained.

"Mary?" Sharon seemed perplexed and then, "Oh, of course, Porkpie, you're Bea's sister. Just a mo," and the head disappeared for a moment or two until the whole of Sharon reappeared at the now opened door.

"You've come about the kittens," she stated and before Porkpie could explain, she disappeared down the hallway saying over her shoulder, "I'll get the key."

A few minutes later the two women were standing outside the door of number 14, gazing at the car parked in the driveway. "That wasn't there yesterday," Sharon said in some surprise, "they must be back already. I thought they were away until the weekend," she added. They stood for a moment, hesitating to ring the doorbell. "It wouldn't do to go barging in now, would it?" Sharon chuckled to herself, "They might be in a state of undress if they're jet-lagged. I must say that I don't recognise that car though. Theirs is blue not green and it's bigger than that one. It's a puzzle…"

She would have prattled on but at that moment she was interrupted by a voice from behind the dividing hedge with number 16. "They're not back. That's their son's car. He's come for the kittens. Apparently, someone has bought all three online. It seems you can sell anything online these days. I hope they're going to good homes." An elderly man appeared at the end of the driveway and smiled cheerfully at the two ladies. "Can I help with anything?" he asked.

As Sharon took her next breath in readiness for a full explanation of their purpose and probably their life histories also, Porkpie spoke quickly, "I wonder if you know anything about the fourth kitten. The one that isn't there," she explained.

"Well now, as it happens, I do know a bit about it," he began. "I was weeding my front garden about ten days ago when I noticed a young girl standing outside number 11" he waved a hand vaguely in the direction of the house opposite his. "She looked a bit lost and upset so I asked if I could help. She was hesitant to talk to me – you know they tell all youngsters not to talk to suspicious looking strangers. Do I look suspicious to you?"

He chuckled to himself but didn't wait for a reply, "I just wanted to cheer her up so I invited her to come into my garden to see the kittens. They often come through the hedge," he explained. "They can get out of next-door's kitchen through the cat-flap. She didn't stay long. Said she had to go somewhere. I did think it was a bit odd for her not to be in school but you never know what kids are up to these days. She was well dressed and looked cared for, so I wasn't worried."

"What was she wearing?" Porkpie interrupted thoughtfully.

"Blue coat, grey skirt. I don't know what else. That's all I remember."

"Thank you. You've been very helpful. If you think of anything else, could you call the marina and ask for Kevin?"

"You're welcome," he said before adding, "I think I've seen her before. Not for a long time you understand but I'm pretty sure she and her mum used to visit the couple at number 11. Sad affair that one. Perhaps that's why she was here then but she didn't stay. I suppose the missing kitten must have followed her wherever she went next."

Sharon and Porkpie bade him farewell and thanked him again for his very helpful information.

What to make of it she wasn't at all sure, but Porkpie was in a hurry to get back to Kevin and share what she had learned. She refused Sharon's offer of a cup of tea and rejected the temptation to peer through the windows of number 11.

It was only as she sat on the bus, willing it to take her home more quickly, that she realised that despite her newfound information, she was no nearer to finding Sophie; neither where she had come from, nor where she had gone.

***

Silently, she cried. How long had she been here? She was colder and hungrier than ever and

92

now she desperately needed the loo. She had no way of knowing whether it was day or night or where she was. She did know she was in a building of some sort and that she was near a railway track. About once every twenty minutes or so (she had no watch to be exact and, in any case, could not have read the time in the darkness) she could hear a train rush by.

When a door banged open and the small space flooded with light, she caught a glimpse of a wooden staircase and an open space beyond the doorway, before all was blotted out again by the figure that descended the stairs and came to a halt in front of her. She looked up at where a face should have been but all she could make out was a large nose and a squashy hat. A woollen scarf covered the mouth and ears, the eyes were hidden behind the brim of the hat and as a blanket was dropped onto her lap the gruff and muffled voice said, "Eat your food. Drink the water. Sleep." And after a pause, "There's a bucket in the corner if you need to go."

Trembling from head to foot, she wanted to ask so many questions but she got no further than, "How long…" when the silhouetted figure turned away and mounted the stairs. Soon the door was locked once more and darkness shrouded everything.

The sandwich tasted good, the water was fresh and the blanket appeared to be clean. 'Small mercies' the wise head on young shoulders reassured; but still there were no answers, no explanation for her current situation.

Chapter 16

He was more disturbed than he cared to admit. It wasn't in his nature to get upset about strange occurrences and he had always adopted the philosophy that people came into and out of one's life where paths crossed and lessons were to be learnt. Sometimes the lesson was for oneself but often it was for the other. It really wasn't that he didn't care; rather that he cared too much but he couldn't afford to let that caring interfere with his work and subsequent pay. As it was, he lived on a shoestring with no room for luxuries and had it not been for the generosity of Pete, the Marina owner, he wouldn't even have been able to use the mooring where he was currently tethered.

He'd finished his work for the day, had fed himself, the cat and the bird, and was preparing for sleep. He couldn't bring himself to use the bed he had made up for Sophie – that was a bit too close to accepting her absence and he fully expected (or rather, hoped) that she would reappear just as unexpectedly as she had arrived in the first place; although, preferably, not so water logged.

"Kevin, are you in there?" Porkpie called softly, "Are you awake?"

He invited her in, hoping she had some good news to share. Of all the people he had come across in his life, she was the only one whose company he didn't object to. Perhaps it was because, in her own slightly odd way, she was as individual as himself and had no expectations of him other than mutual respect for their personal idiosyncrasies and a joint caring for the half-drowned girl they had rescued.

The little grey cat wound itself round her legs before clambering up onto her lap as she perched on the edge of the sofa-bed sipping a mug of cocoa. "It's about this little furry thing," she began and went on to tell Kevin all that the gentleman at number 16 had explained.

"The thing is," she went on, "I think it might give us a clue as to where she came from. If what he said about her visiting the people at number 11 is accurate, then perhaps that's where we should try next."

"But didn't you say that the woman was dead? Murdered or something," Kevin was doubtful and always reluctant to involve other people in his business.

"Hmm, yes, and the man, her husband or partner, whichever he was, is, as I understand it, something of a drinker. I doubt we'd get much sense from him." It seemed that they had hit another brick wall in their attempts to solve this particular problem, "But at least we know where this little being came from. Do you think we should take her back?"

"No!" Kevin answered rather more sharply than she had expected. He had become used to the feline presence in his boat and together with the bird he had begun to think of them as his 'family'.

Somehow, they both had a connection with Sophie and if they were still there then he could hold on to his expectation of her return – when she was ready, of course.

"Well, if you're going to keep them both, I think they need names, wouldn't you agree? You can't really go on calling them 'cat' and 'bird'," she chuckled.

He looked at her in surprise, "Why not? That is what they are isn't it? In any case, I can't keep the bird for ever, it's a wild creature and needs to be back with its own kind. I'm just waiting for it to be strong enough to fly again."

A short time later, having got no further with their plans to find Sophie, and having sat for a while in companionable silence, sipping their cocoa, Porkpie stood up. The cat slid to the floor and scampered off into the bedroom. Kevin also rose to his feet and held out a somewhat formal hand for his visitor to shake.

"Oh, come here, you big softie." Porkpie pulled him awkwardly into her arms and hugged him warmly. Once he had recovered from his astonishment at her demonstrative affection, he patted her back as a man will often do when hugging another man; brother or father perhaps. He muttered, "Bye for now then," and she, a little embarrassed, laughed lightly and replied, "Good night," as she left and, "see you later!" What she didn't see was the tear that he brushed away with the back of his hand.

***

Wilfred had sat in the pub for far too long. As usual he was significantly inebriated although not completely comatose. He had watched other customers come and go until it was almost closing time. He was reluctant to go home. The house had become cold, too quiet and it felt empty without Milly's presence. Despite that she hadn't always been pleased to see him and had rarely spoken a nice word to him in recent times, she had been ever present and she was undoubtedly a home-maker. Since her death, he had only eaten TV dinners or take-aways – that is when he bothered to eat at all. His bed remained unmade and the curtains closed. Hence, he preferred the dubious company of the regulars at the Pig and Whistle rather than his own thoughts and memories.

Usually, the punters were the same people who drank, either together or alone, and who would nod to him in recognition as they passed his barstool in the corner. He couldn't exactly say he knew them but he recognised their faces and knew their habits. On this particular evening there had been one or two newcomers to take his notice and for some reason or other he had noted a couple of men who sat in a corner booth with their heads close together and talking urgently and privately.

Once or twice the younger of the two looked up in his direction and, for a brief moment as their eyes met, Wilfred thought perhaps he recognised the man. The second man wore a khaki hat which was squashy and pulled down low over his brow. Most of the time his back was turned toward Wilfred but just once he glanced over his shoulder and swiftly took in the old sot who swayed slightly as he tipped back his glass to sup the dregs of his tipple.

As he made his way unsteadily past the booths and tables near the exit door, he overheard, "Shouldn't be too difficult to get rid of him but she's another matter altogether."

***

It was the banging of a door that woke her. For a moment, she wondered where she was but realisation came quickly and she sat up in the pitch-black listening for further noises.

'Voices; two, male' she noted before the rumble of a train drowned out any other sounds. Briefly, once the train had gone by, she heard footsteps which appeared to be directly overhead. There was the scrape of something being pulled across a wooden floor and then… nothing.

She pulled the blanket more tightly about her shoulders and tried to go back to sleep. Surely something would happen tomorrow? There must be some reason why she was stuck down here. Who was the squashy hatted man who had thrown a bag over her head and carried her out and away from Kevin's boat?

She wished with all her heart that she was back in the cosy cabin with Kevin, Aunty Pie, the crow and the little grey cat.

Chapter 17

It had been a long first week back at school. It always took a few days for the routine to swing into gear and of course the summer term included more changes to the timetable than from winter to spring. There were swimming lessons and outdoor activities as well as the year 6 SATs exams, which were heartily hated by staff and pupils alike; and then the school trip for the leavers as well as a concert or play for the parents, to be organised. Mrs Wells sighed as she made her way back to her office having seen the last of the children off the premises and out through the front gate. Now she must address the issue of the absentees before beginning her own foreshortened weekend.

She was aware that she really ought to have dealt with one particular missing child at the end of the previous term but she had hoped that the situation would resolve itself and the girl would reappear this week. However, she had not and so it was time to draw her absence to the attention of the child attendance officer at County Hall. It was not unusual for parents to take their offspring away for a holiday during term time and although it was frowned upon by the authorities and recorded as an unauthorised absence, Mrs Wells, having been a parent of young children herself, was inclined to turn a blind eye to occasionally missing pupils.

There were, of course, repeated offenders of whom she was also well aware. Frankie Wood had been a prime example until he had made friends with Billy Frost. Frankie's mother had health problems of her own. His father was a long-distance lorry driver and consequently there had been many occasions when Frankie was obliged to stay at home to care for his mum. Fortunately, a coincidental combination of Frankie's desire to spend time with Billy and his father's redundancy had culminated in the resolution of that specific problem.

Mrs Wells had been pleased to welcome Tilda into year 6. She was a delightful and well-behaved child who had settled well with her foster carer. Mrs Wells had known Carol for many years and had met her several times when she welcomed Carol's fosterlings into the reception class once they were old enough for 'proper' school.

Although Tilda was older than Carol's usual clientele, Mrs Wells was aware of the tragedy, a couple of years ago, that had befallen a little boy that Carol had cared for. No wonder poor Carol had suffered some sort of breakdown and how nice it was to see her smiling and confident again with Tilda in tow.

That afternoon, Tilda had waylaid Mrs Wells as she crossed the playground to reprimand a child who was hanging upside down from the rickety climbing frame (she really ought to get rid of that old thing before someone seriously hurt themselves!)

"Excuse me," the child politely but tentatively began, "I was wondering if you know someone called Sophie?" Tilda went on to explain that she had a friend called Sophie whom she had met at a party for a mutual playmate, "She told me that her school was called St Cecilia's so when Aunty Carol said I was coming here, I was hoping I might see her again. But she hasn't been here at all this week. Did she leave and go somewhere else?"

There it was; the prompt that she had needed to insist that she do something about the absentee child. Mrs Wells reassured the worried child that as far as she was aware, Sophie had not left the school. She thanked Tilda for reminding her to make some enquiries and promised to let her know as soon as had something to tell.

**

"What happened to your report from last week when you went to check up on the girl on a boat?" Wendy had been rummaging through the file box having failed to find anything in the computer records. She wasn't at all trusting of the PC system and much preferred good old-fashioned paper-work.

Burly Bob looked up from whatever it was he was studiously perusing on his desk and with a slightly bemused expression declared, "I'm sure I gave it to you. Are you sure it isn't on your desk?"

Wendy turned to her immaculately tidy desk and scowled at her partner, "Do you see it on there?"

Her sarcastic response was not unexpected, she certainly didn't suffer fools gladly and there were times when Bob could be particularly foolish. "You did fill in a report sheet, didn't you?" Her glare was enough to freeze an iceberg and without waiting for a reply she continued, "I think the girl in question was called Susie or Sammy or something similar…"

"Sophie," Bob muttered, "but why does it matter so much at this time on a Friday?" he asked. To his mind it was definitely time to call it a day. He had an appointment with his own children, it being his weekend; one in every three, when he got to spend time with the twins whilst their mother, his wife of course, visited her family whose company was a total anathema to him.

"It matters because I think I may have made a connection," Wendy retorted.

"What sort of connection?" Bob was gradually becoming more interested and dug into his pocket for his now dry but still muddied notebook. Soon two heads were bowed over the almost illegible account which Bob began to decipher as best he could, in combination with his memory of the less than pleasant experience of talking to that irascible older lady; Mary something, he seemed to recall.

The final outcome of their trying to make something of the muddied page was that Bob had not, in fact, actually seen the girl at all and had come to the misguided conclusion that she was attending school just as that Mary-pie lady had implied. "Why on earth didn't you go back later in the day to check again that the girl was living there as claimed?" Wendy was quietly fuming; she could be in all sorts of trouble with head office for not taking suitable safeguarding procedures concerning the young girl.

"It was that day when I was sick. I'd eaten too many doughnuts. Remember? Then I forgot – because I hadn't seen anything troublesome," Bob was both indignant and ashamed which made him feel very uncomfortable. Red-faced and rather shaky, he was about to ask if he could go home – if there was nothing else he could assist with, when Wendy saved him the bother, "Oh go away! Get out of my sight, you useless lump of lard…" Silently fuming at the insult, he left as quickly as he could although he slammed the door with enough force to make a very satisfying bang, thus demonstrating just how upset he actually was.

Wendy decided that she would go home via the marina and hope that at least one of the occupants of the shabby canal boat could throw some light on the whereabouts of the girl. Part of her irritation with Bob was misdirected ire since she was also annoyed with herself for her perfunctory dismissal of Miss Mary Milliner's visit earlier that week. She would have to apologise to him and probably to her too…

Chapter 18

He wasn't exactly comfortable, sitting in the solicitor's opulent office. One way and another, he'd had rather too much to do with the law. He had managed to avoid a custodial sentence but he'd been obliged to wear a curfew tracker and obey a restriction order as well as completing certain community service projects. It had been largely due to that bitch of a woman who had brought a complaint against him. Well, she was out of the picture now and so was her interfering mother. That just left the kid and he had plans to deal with her. He smirked to himself as the anticipation of a nice fat windfall warmed his cold heart. He would show them all that he wasn't someone to be trifled with; they would come crawling to him for assistance in the not-too-distant future.

He was satisfied that the man he had hired to help him execute his plan, was trustworthy – at least as far as any criminal, only interested in money, can be trusted, but there would be plenty of dosh to keep him happy once this was all over and done with and in any case the man owed him a favour.

What he hadn't accounted for was the old man. His face fell as the solicitor read aloud the contents of a manilla envelope. "Bugger," he thought to himself, "There's always someone to f*** it all up. Now I'll have to find a way of getting rid of him too." He smiled vaguely and unconvincingly at the suited lawyer, thanked him perfunctorily and left, closing the door a little more firmly than was strictly necessary as he did so.

***

Wilfred was astonished. He asked the solicitor to repeat his words several times before they began to sink in. At first, he could only assimilate snippets of information; stop drinking, dry for at least six months, right to stay in the property and something about money or income.

"Would you like me to write down the details and send them to you, sir?" the lawyer waited for his dishevelled and confused client to respond.

"Erm, run it by me one more time if you don't mind; it's a lot to take in!"

"Right, of course. But I think I'll write it down anyway so you can go over it again in your own time."

Wilfred nodded and listened carefully as the kindly solicitor read the contents once more.

"The house is yours, on condition that you stop drinking and remain sober for at least six months from today's date. You will be provided with enough money to pay the bills and feed yourself until such time as you are able to acquire a job and income of your own, as long as that time is no more than one year from today's date. You have the right to remain in the property for one year, but only if you conform to the conditions indicated.

After one year you must be in a position to support yourself or the house will be sold and the proceeds shared between you and Mrs Martin's granddaughter. The granddaughter (when she can be located) is to be cared for by Social Services until such time as you or her absentee father are able to look after her or until she comes of age. It was Mrs Martin's wish that the child be reconciled with her father but, realistically, she understood that that seemed unlikely given his extended absence. In the meantime, the child will be made a ward of court and will have suitable decisions and arrangements made for her until she is eighteen years old."

"She didn't say anything more about her son-in-law?"

The lawyer looked surprised at first and then turned a little red, "Well, as it happens," he blustered, "someone came to see me this morning, claiming to be Mrs Martin's son-in-law. I've told him the same as I told you but he needs to verify his identity before I can disclose more precise details. Nevertheless, he isn't mentioned in the Will except where the granddaughter is concerned. However, I had the distinct impression that Mrs Martin didn't expect the man to appear. We can't be too careful when dealing with legacy and inheritance and I have several enquiries to make before a positive judgement. The first and most important of those factors is the whereabouts of your granddaughter. I don't suppose you have any idea, do you?"

"Step-granddaughter," Wilfred corrected, "and no, I haven't seen her for quite a long time. Last I heard, she was being difficult for her mum but that was just after the little boy died and before the mum took her own life. Pretty terrible state of affairs really. I'm not surprised the girl ran away," and then as an afterthought, "I'd like to know what happened to her though. She was a good kid but there wasn't much left for her to stay around here for, poor girl." It was a sincere declaration and for the first time Wilfred felt inclined to attempt to do what his late wife had dictated. He would try to dry out. He would clean himself up. He would even try to trace the little girl; after all, they only had each other left now.

He almost habitually turned in to the Pig and Whistle on his way home but instead, resisting the temptation, he went to the fish and chip shop and bought himself a nice piece of cod and mushy peas. He'd pop into the corner shop and get some milk too; he might have to make do with tea and coffee if this thing was really going to work.

***

After his two morning clients had left, the solicitor stretched his aching back, scratched his head and pressed the intercom buzzer to ask his secretary to bring him some coffee. There had been rather a lot to take in and due to the extraordinary circumstances, he felt the need to think things through in detail and get his facts straight. What had seemed to be a fairly straightforward probate was becoming complicated in the extreme!

Mrs Martin had come to see him about three years previously. She hadn't revised her will since her first husband had died several years before then. Because her second husband had proven to be something of a habitual alcoholic, she had been concerned to ensure that he didn't drink away any remaining capital and that her daughter and granddaughter were provided for but without leaving Wilfred with no home and no money. Hence, the conditions attached to the legacy. However, the situation had changed rather dramatically when her daughter's husband had left her and, following the tragic death of little Alfie, the daughter, having teamed up with an abusive and controlling second partner, had consequently committed suicide.

"What an incredible series of unfortunate events," Paul mused aloud to himself and sighed just as Helen, his assistant, came through the door with his coffee. "Sounds as though you have something of a problem to solve," she commented. "Anything I can help with?"

"Hmm…" at first, he was dubious, but then, "Perhaps two heads would be better than one," he surmised, and he repeated the situation to her. The more times he explained it, the more complicated it seemed to become. "Where to begin?" and he threw wide his arms with upturned hands.

"At the beginning." Helen, looking at the problem with fresh eyes, suggested that there were two things to address immediately. One was the verification of the supposed son-in-law's identity and the second was the whereabouts of the granddaughter. The release of funds in support of Wilfred Martin was already set in motion so there was no further need to do anything in that quarter – other than monitoring his drinking habits and even that was largely up to him.

By the end of the afternoon, Paul went home satisfied that the local constabulary were on the case with regards to the identity of the man claiming to be Mrs Martin's son-in-law and Helen had made an appointment with Wendy Crispin of Social Services regarding the whereabouts of Sophie Clarkson.

Chapter 19

The crow perched on the edge of the opened cage door. It's head on one side, it gazed steadily at the little grey cat who crouched, ready to spring, in the gangway between the galley and the main cabin. It being late April and outside temperatures regularly reaching double figures, Kevin had not lit the squat stove for several days. Apart from anything else, he barely spent any time at home other than to eat an evening meal and to sleep. There was, if anything, far too much work to be done at this time of year and he had spent the whole day sourcing wood, glues, nails, rivets, paints and varnishes with which to fix and polish the various crafts awaiting his attention. He usually enjoyed his work but this year his mind was distracted by the continuing puzzle of Sophie and her whereabouts.

Yesterday evening, Wendy Crispin, that nice social lady, had turned up as he got home from work and she'd asked a lot more questions about where Sophie had come from and what, if anything, she had said about her previous life. He had told her all that he knew; that she had obviously been badly treated at times, that she had seemed happy enough staying on the boat with him and Mary Milliner, that the little cat had arrived with her but she had said nothing about where it had come from and didn't seem to know any more than that it had followed her and saved her when she fell in the water.

She hadn't intended to drown herself but had slipped and fallen unintentionally into the river. She had been reluctant to talk about anything other than the immediate but was keen to learn all about the boats, wildlife and nature. All in all, there was nothing very helpful he could add to what Porkpie had already told the gentleman social worker who had come earlier and the police who constantly reminded them that there were no reports of a missing child.

The following day was a Sunday and even though there was plenty of work he ought to be getting on with, he had promised Porkpie that they would go over the events of the last few days to see if they could throw any light on the potential whereabouts of Sophie. Promptly at ten in the morning, there was a light rap on the cabin roof and, "Can I come in?" called Porkpie. Kevin was rather surprised when behind her sister, Beanie came awkwardly down the steps and into the boat.

"I hope you don't mind," Porkpie was apologetic, "but Bea thought she might be able to help too. Especially after she found out about the little cat. Have you named it yet?" changing the subject served to nip any potential irritation in the bud as Kevin replied, "No. I thought Sophie should do that. It's her cat after all."

"Right; fair enough. So where shall we begin?" Before they could say anything more,

114

Beanie spoke up, "I really think it has something to do with that squashy hat that I told you about."

"Oh, hush Bea," Porkpie spoke sharply, "you don't even know for certain that you saw anyone. You just think you did. I'm sure it was just your overactive imagination."

"Wait a minute," Kevin was not so quick to dismiss Beanie's suggestion. "Tell me a bit more about this squashy person."

Beatrice did not need further encouragement and she told them of the number of times that she had noticed the distinctive hat; sometimes hiding behind a hedge, sometimes walking briskly away and on the last occasion, running as best it could from Kevin's boat.

"Did you actually see someone step off the boat?" Kevin was almost convinced.

"No, but they were right next to it and carrying something heavy. It could have been the girl but I couldn't swear to it. Mary is right," she continued sadly, "it wouldn't hold up in a court of law."

"Just as well we're not in a court then," Porkpie was softening towards her sister's idea; mainly because they had absolutely nothing else to go on. "Which way did you say he went?"

"Away from us and towards the marina moorings and office." Silence ensued until...

"That's it!" Both Beanie and her sister almost jumped out of their skins at Kevin's shout. The cat shot into the bedroom and the bird flapped off the door and into the relative safety of the cage.

"What is?" Porkpie spoke first and Kevin replied, "CCTV." The women were puzzled. "What is that?" asked Beanie.

"You know, those cameras they have on buildings for security and suchlike," Porkpie had cottoned on to Kevin's line of thought, "Of course!" she exclaimed, "Why didn't we think about that before?" There was no need to answer the rhetorical question but her next query had them all scratching their heads. "How do we get to see it?"

The ensuing silence was palpable until Kevin stood up and silently reached for the kettle which he filled and put on the hob to boil. Tea was often a good starting point when trying to resolve a situation.

Mugs in hands and thoughts spinning, the three were still silent as they each tried to think of a way to access the CCTV recordings. After about another ten minutes, Kevin spoke first, "I know that the cameras were installed by a security company. I should imagine that there must be a label of some sort on some of the equipment. I don't think it's monitored from within the office so it must go to an outside recording device somewhere or other. If I can find a way to reach one of the cameras, I might be able to find a contact number or at least the name of the equipment supplier or maker."

"What is the point of having cameras if you can't access what they record?" A perfectly reasonable question from Beanie but, "I think they are there as much for a deterrent as they might be for recording a crime," Porkpie surmised. "This is a pretty 'safe' area with not much crime to worry about." Kevin thought about the number of times he had left his own boat unlocked with no thought at all for potential burglars or other crimes such as vandalism. If only he had locked it when Sophie was inside…

It was agreed once the Sunday and weekend boaters had finished for the day they would go to the office, which was closed on a Sunday, and see how accessible the camera was; the one that pointed down the towpath towards Kevin's boat. He was of the opinion that it was mounted high up on a telegraph pole that carried the electricity lines to the various moorings and would therefore be potentially quite dangerous to try and access. In the meantime, Beanie and Porkpie would go for a stroll round the marina to see if they could locate a more easily accessible camera with, hopefully, an informative sticker of some sort on it.

They all felt much better having something positive to work on and think about. Nevertheless, what to do with any information that they might glean from such a source was another matter.

***

It was unbearably quiet in the very small space at the bottom of a wooden staircase. Her tears had dried up long ago and her head was empty of any emotion other than a longing to be out of this place. The trains still rumbled by but less frequently, "It must be Sunday," she thought and calculated that she had been in this situation for about four days. She wasn't cold, she wasn't hungry, she had got used to turning off feelings and desires when that man, Dave had abused her so cruelly. It wasn't worth wanting anything 'cos you weren't going to get it anyway. However, she couldn't turn off the wanting to be out of there and, further, wanting her mum. And, above all, wanting things to be as they used to be a long time ago; before Alfie died, before Dad left, before Dave came and before Mum changed. Another tear trickled down her cheek despite her determination to not cry any more, and she curled up into a foetal position and pulled the blanket over her head. She wouldn't cry, she wouldn't think, she would just wait for something, anything to change.

Chapter 20

Something was niggling at the back of DI Evans' mind. It had been an odd sort of week filled with several insignificant issues, as well as the overriding importance of the death of Mrs Martin. There would, of course, have to be an autopsy and an inquest into her untimely demise, but he was confident in his own opinion that it had been a very unfortunate accident. The woman had been either getting down or putting away a large vase when she had lost her balance, dropped the vase and then fallen from the stool she was perched on, onto the broken glass which had cut her carotid artery. She would have died very quickly – small mercies, but in this job, you often had to look on the bright side in order to retain your own sanity.

The niggle was something to do with the various items found in Mrs Martin's house. There were all the usual knickknacks, holiday memorabilia, ornaments and bits and pieces but there were no photographs on display. Mr Martin had mentioned a daughter and a son when he was interviewed shortly after the accident, but the investigators and forensic people had found no references to either. As well as those comments, there were the two small boys who had found the body; hadn't they said something about the woman baking cookies for someone? Could that have anything to do with her family? Visiting her perhaps

– but why no pictures? That surely is quite unusual…he decided that first thing tomorrow morning he would go and see Wilfred Martin, since there were definitely some unresolved issues in this case and the man hadn't been exactly open and forthcoming when interviewed earlier. There had been rather a lot of alcohol involved, Evans seemed to recall.

***

"You're tired, my dear!" Mr Wells noted the dark rings under his wife's eyes and the furrowed brow above them. She sighed deeply. "Anything I can help with?" he asked.

"I don't think so," she replied, "unless you can solve the mystery of a missing girl whom nobody seems to have missed,"

"Tell me about it?" he invited and then, "Have you reported it to the School Attendance Officer?" Mrs Wells replied in the affirmative and went on to explain that they had assured her they would go to the girls registered address first thing on Monday morning.

"Then what are you worrying about? It sounds as though you've done all that you can."

She smiled at him, grateful for his encouraging support, but continued to explain that she had had concerns about this particular girl in the past. There had been unexplained absences before as well as nasty bruising on some occasions. She now wished that she had investigated more thoroughly. It was sometimes very difficult to get right the balance between protecting and interfering.

"There was also a particularly harrowing time just after a terrible accident in which the younger brother was killed. Sophie missed several weeks of school then, but the bruises didn't start appearing until sometime afterwards." She sighed again and there was a short pause before, "I really wish I'd noted her absence before the Easter break. As it is, I didn't react quickly enough. It took the prompting of another pupil before I did something positive." Another pause and a tear wiped away, "Perhaps it's time I thought about taking that retirement…"

***

Just as darkness fell, a strange threesome made their way as quietly as possible down the towpath towards the marina. Kevin walked in front and Porkpie brought up the rear. Between them Beanie waddled along, unused to being out and about at this time of the day. She was much more of a home bird and was trying very hard to not mind missing her usual Sunday evening viewing on the TV. Kevin carried a collapsible ladder, Beanie; a torch and Porkpie had a notepad and pen. Earlier that day she and her sister had noticed a camera mounted on the top of the gatepost at the entrance to the marina. At this time, the gate would be closed and locked; only those who knew the code could punch it in to the electronic keypad and thereby gain access to their own craft. The code was changed regularly and so, together with the CCTV rig, the marina was secure with the only other access being from the towpath which was accessible on foot or by bicycle. The nearest road access to the path was about a mile from where Kevin's boat was moored on the outer edge of the marina and, therefore, a good three quarters of a mile from the Milliner sister's cabin.

Kevin stopped. Beanie bumped into his broad back and Porkpie almost tripped over Beanie's abruptly halted figure. "There's someone out there on the road side of the fence," he whispered.

"Why are we whispering?" asked Beanie and at the same time, "Does it matter if we're seen? We're not doing anything illegal!" Porkpie was the only one to speak out loud.

"Good evening!" called the outsider, "I'm looking for someone called Mary. Do you know her?"

"No!"

"What?"

"Why?"

All three answered at the same time. The stranger looked a little perplexed as he pushed a peaked hat away from his brow, "Well, if you happen to come across her, would you give her a message please?" and without waiting for a response, "tell her Sharon sent me and I might know something about that girl Mary was asking about. I'm staying at the Pig and Whistle for a few nights if you want to find me."

And with that, he was gone. The three investigators were left in stunned silence; wordlessly staring at each other. Eventually Beanie broke the spell by pointing at the sign affixed to the gatepost and said, "There it is." Without replying, Kevin extended his ladder, leant it against the gatepost and carefully climbed up. When he was high enough, Beanie stretched up to hand him the torch and Porkpie stood with pen poised over paper waiting for him to read out any significant details.

A short while later, the motley but satisfied trio could be seen making their way back to the boat and beyond to their cosy cabin. They were now armed with a telephone number which purported to offer assistance to anyone noticing anything suspicious about the security installation. That should at the very least give them a starting point in their mission to discover whether Squashy hat had been carrying Sophie away from the boat.

Just as Beanie was drifting off to sleep, Porkpie called from her room across the corridor, "Did you notice anything about that man?"

"What man?"

"The man at the gate,"

"What sort of anything?"

"Well, I might be wrong, but I thought he looked a bit like Sophie!" Beanie was about to respond when her sister's sleepy voice muttered,

"How silly of me. Of course, you haven't met Sophie yet!"

Chapter 21

He missed the camaraderie of his fellow drinkers in the Pig and Whistle. His neighbour, Sharon, had been a tower of strength in helping him to stick to his promise and she always had a lot of gossip to share with anyone who was willing to listen, but generally speaking, it wasn't the sort of information he was interested in discussing. She'd brought him many home-cooked meals and even took his washing away to sort out and return freshy laundered. She had also been wonderful in disposing of Milly's clothes and personal belongings.

However, on this particular morning, he felt that if he had to listen to yet another report on this person's new baby or that child's misdeeds, Mrs So-and-so's recalcitrant dog or Mr Thingamy's job loss, he might scream. Therefore, Monday morning found him in his usual corner at the bar, nursing a glass of Coca-Cola. Nelly, the barmaid, had also been very understanding when he had explained why he wasn't taking his usual tipple and even, when he had been tempted to break his vow to stay 'dry', refused to serve him and gave him sparkling water instead.

She greeted him warmly and chatted amicably while she wiped down the tables and benches in readiness for the regular punters. "There's been one or two new people since you last came in," she announced, "We've even had one chap staying here for a few nights. He seems very nice but a bit out of touch with what's been going on in this part of the world. Says he's been overseas for a couple of years. You just missed him this morning but I expect he'll be back a bit later on. Said he had a few things to sort out while he's here."

Her attention was taken by another early customer but after serving the newcomer she came back to chat with Wilfred, "There's been another odd sort of bloke been in a few times. He wears a squashy sort of hat and always looks a bit scruffy. His friend is much younger and seems a bit bossy. I don't like them much so I'm glad they never stay very long."

Nelly continued alternately serving and chatting and Wilfred relaxed into the familiarity of the pub atmosphere. "It's odd," he mused, "how different things are when you look at the world through sober eyes. Things seem more intense somehow; funny is funnier, happy is happier but then again, sad is sadder and bad is truly awful." He found himself thinking about Milly's accidental death and tears dripped down into his cola; he thought about little Alfie and his mum – both deaths were so unnecessary; especially Julie's.

It was whilst he was thinking about Julie that the squashy hatted man entered the bar, closely followed by… "Well, I never! Would you believe it? That's Dave, the disgrace of a man young Julie teamed up with after Alfie's accident. Even though I was half-cut most of the time, I didn't like him from the start." Nelly looked at him in surprise, "Are you sure?" she asked.

"I couldn't swear to it, but I'm pretty certain it's him."

"What about the other chap?"

"Never seen him before," and after a pause, "Actually, I think I did see him in here, last time I had a proper drink." For a brief moment he was tempted to go over to the couple and say a word or two; some home truths perhaps, to that reprobate and apology for a man, but realising he had no Dutch courage to help him stand up to the wretch, he changed his mind telling himself that the man just wasn't worth it. In any case the damage was done; Julie was dead and the little girl was nowhere to be found.

Had he ventured nearer to the two heads bent close and low, he might have overheard and perhaps have been forewarned of what was to befall him later that day but as it happened, he left by the back door and made his way home for lunch.

It was mid-afternoon when he awoke with a start from the involuntary nap his full belly had imposed upon him. The knock came again; with greater urgency this time. He struggled to his feet and shuffled to open the door. He must be getting old; he thought, now when did that happen?

He didn't recognise the younger man standing on his doorstep, a salesman perhaps, "Afternoon, how can I help you?"

"Don't you know me?" the visitor replied and as Wilfred peered up into his face, "I'm Steven, I was Milly's son-in-law; Sophie and Alfie's dad."

"Well, I never," for the second time that day Wilfred was almost lost for words, "Come in, come in," he opened the door wide and welcomed him in.

"I'm so sorry for what happened to Milly," Steven began, "Your neighbour explained," he clarified, "She was always kind to me and I felt bad about abandoning her as well as the others when things went sour between me and Julie. I tried to keep in touch for the kids' but then I just couldn't cope with what happened to Al…" his voice broke as he couldn't bring himself to say his son's name. "Anyway, I went abroad; trying to run away from myself I suppose. I always meant to come back for Sophie's sake but things conspired to stop me. About a fortnight ago I received an official looking letter from the coroner's office telling me about Julie taking her own life. If only I'd known how bad things had become, especially with that no-good Dave that Julie hooked up with." He paused for breath and to gather his thoughts. Wilfred, realising how difficult this was for Sophie's dad, waited patiently to know what it was that was wanted of him.

At last, "Anyhow, I came as soon as I could get a flight but what I really came here for was to ask whether you know where Sophie is? I've been to the house but it's all boarded up and I don't know where she might go to school or who any of her friends are. I don't even know what she looks like now." His breath caught in his throat and he coughed to disguise the sob that threatened to escape him. Then, after a pause, "Your neighbour told me that a lady who lives near the marina, had mentioned a little girl. I went there to ask yesterday evening, but the gate to the place was locked. I spoke to some odd-looking people who were doing something by the gate but they didn't know who I was talking about. Or if they did, they didn't say so."

Wilfred was ashamed to admit that he hadn't given the girl a minute's thought. He'd been far too wrapped up in his own misery when he wasn't drowned in his cups, and, of course, Milly wasn't there to think about her either. Now he was obliged to tell this man that he, the only person left in Sophie's life, had absolutely no idea where she had gone. If he could have fallen through the floor, he would have prayed for it to open up and swallow him but since no such saving graces exist in reality, he hung his head in shame and told her father that he hadn't seen Sophie since before her mother, and now her grandmother, had died.

No sooner had the words left his lips, when there was a loud crashing sound that appeared to come from the kitchen. Both men leapt to their feet and cautiously made their way to see what had caused the interruption.

There on the floor, amidst much broken window glass, was a brick with a piece of paper wrapped round it and held in place by a couple of elastic bands.

Steven was on the point of telling Wilfred not to touch anything when the latter had already removed the bands, unfolded the paper and read aloud, "If you value your granddaughter's life, come to the old mill at 7.00pm. Come alone. Any police or such-like and she will be punished."

Chapter 22

For the fourth time, Paul Winger, LLB, scrutinised the document that he held in his shaking hand and wondered about the implications of the information written therein.

"Our investigations show that Dave Clarkson, formerly known as David Clark, changed his name by deed poll at the same time as he began co-habiting with Julie Clarkson of Topstreet Way, Hartford. A request to adopt the two children abiding at the same address was denied on the grounds of their father neither having deceased nor being contactable to either agree or disagree to the removal of his parental rights in favour of Mr Dave Clarkson. Mr D Clarkson was advised to wait until such time as contact was made with Mr S Clarkson or until five years had elapsed at which time, assuming there had been no word from Mr S Clarkson, he could reapply to the courts."

There it was in black and white. Dave Clarkson was not the legal son-in-law of Mrs Milly Martin and, therefore, not entitled to any inheritance from her estate. Ergo; Mr Martin would inherit the house and on his eventual demise, it would pass to the granddaughter, "who is yet to be found!"

"Pardon?" Helen had been concentrating on her own work, "What did you say?" she repeated.

"He's not going to like it but he's going to have to accept it!"

"Who and what?"

"Mr Clarkson…"

"Oh," she interrupted before he had finished his sentence, "you mean Steve, he rang earlier and left you a message."

"Steve?" Paul was now thoroughly confused, "No, his name is Dave or David. Anyway, he's not going to like the fact that he's not a beneficiary in the Martin probate case."

It was Helen's turn to be confused, "There's something a bit crazy going on here," she said, "I went to school with Steve Clarkson and I'd recognise his voice anywhere. He rang this morning to say he needed to talk to you about his daughter, Sophie. He said she's missing and that he was going to the police station first but then he needs to see you to find out the contents of his mother-in-law's will."

***

DI Evans stood on Wilfred's doorstep and knocked sharply on the dolphin shaped brass doorknocker. A few minutes later shuffling footsteps could be heard coming towards the door and a beslippered and pyjamaed old man opened the door and invited him in. "G'morning, officer," he respectfully uttered, "How can I help you today?" and before the DI could respond, "Come to check on whether I've been drinking? Hmm? I haven't!"

and he held out his mug of strong black coffee in evidence of his claim.

"No; nothing to do with that," Evans assured the man, "I just wanted to ask you a couple more questions. I noticed the other day that you don't have any photographs on display. I find that a little unusual in a family home. Can you explain the absence?"

"That's an easy one to answer," Wilfred almost grinned at the visitor, "my wife…" his breath caught in his throat as he spoke, "I mean my late wife, Millie," he explained, "well she'd had a tough time with her family recently. Her son went abroad a few years ago and he hasn't bothered to be in touch since. I think he's in Canada but actually he could be anywhere. He and his mother never really saw eye to eye and they had an almighty argument the day before he left. His older sister, Julie; well, you know what happened to her," he looked up at the still standing officer who noted the tear that spilled from Wilfred's eye, "She was a good girl but she fell in with a bad lot. I'll never understand how she could take her own life and leave that poor little girl all alone. And now we don't even know where Sophie's gone." Overcome with his own grief, the old man blew his nose noisily into a rather grubby looking handkerchief.

"The photos?" Evans gently prompted.

"She took them all down. They're in a box somewhere. She was going to stick them all into an album so she could look at them when she felt stronger. Trouble is she didn't feel strong enough even to do the sticking. I can get them if you like," he offered.

"I'd just like a picture of the little girl, Sophie. Her absence is becoming serious and I think we must treat this as a missing child case. I'm a bit sorry we haven't done so already but her name has come up several times recently. I need you to tell me as much as you know about the girl."

A short while later, with a photograph tucked carefully into his inside pocket, DI Evans made his way back to the station.

Wilfred stood at his door for some time, watching the unmarked car leave the end of Meadow Walk. He'd been very tempted to say something about the brick through his window and the message that came with it. However, it specifically said 'no police, come alone' and so that's how it must be – except he might take Steve with him. "After all, Sophie is his daughter and not any blood relation of mine…"

***

Beanie was delighted with her own sleuth work. She could hardly wait to tell Porkpie what she had learned about the security company. Apparently, their cameras were all linked to the local police station who would only look at the footage if there was a suggestion of some wrongdoing. The cameras recorded five days at a time and then they overwrote the first day and then the second and so on, so there were only ever five days' worth of filming available to view. Therefore, it was very important that they got hold of the tapes before last Thursday was overwritten.

Unable to sit still whilst she waited for Porkpie to return from trying to find that man at the Pig and Whistle, Beanie decided to make a batch of muffins for whomsoever would like to eat some.

***

"He went out early this morning," Nelly told her apologetically, "I don't know where he went, I'm afraid, but he said he'd be back later and he's still booked in for a couple more nights."

Porkpie thanked the barmaid and turned to leave. She needed to get back to Beanie in order to find out what she had managed to discover. Just as she reached the door it was flung open roughly and she was almost knocked from her feet. She fell against the back of a chair and a rough hand grabbed her arm to prevent her from crashing right to the floor.

"Sorry ma'am," he spoke gruffly, "but you should look where you're going."

"Me look?" she was indignant as well as somewhat shocked, and was preparing to give the man a mouthful about his rude manners when she noticed his hat. It was khaki, floppy and SQUASHY. He held it screwed up in his hand where he had whisked it off his head in a show of gentlemanliness. Completely thrown off balance, both physically and mentally, "No problem. Sorry," she muttered and swiftly went out through the door that he now held open for her.

What to do? Beanie had described the hat exactly and Porkpie was absolutely certain that was the same hat and therefore, logically, the same wearer. Should she 'beard the lion in his den' and confront him about Sophie's whereabouts? But then, if he were up to no good, he would deny all knowledge of the girl, wouldn't he? Perhaps she should ring the police; there was a public phone inside the pub, but that would mean going back in and she didn't want to bring any more attention to herself.

As she was standing stock still just outside the pub door trying to decide what course of action to follow, suddenly Kevin was striding purposefully toward her. "Beanie said you'd be here," he explained matter-of-factly, "She couldn't wait for you to go back so she came to find me. I was at home thank goodness. She told me what she'd found out about the security cameras and now we have to go to the police station."

"Why? I mean what for?" Porkpie was puzzled.

"No time to explain, just come with me and I'll tell you on the way." Kevin took her arm and hurried her down the road to where his pick-up was parked and before long, they stopped outside the police station and were surprised to see firstly, the man who had accosted them from outside the gates the previous night and for whom Porkpie had been searching. Secondly, a smartly dressed man carrying a briefcase and thirdly, Wendy Crispin, the social worker who had ruffled Porkpie's feathers once or twice already.

Further to an early telephone call from the schools' attendance officer at County Hall, and a brief conversation with Mrs Wells at St Cecilia's School, Wendy's growing concern about the whereabouts of a mysterious girl who had appeared (apparently half drowned, in the river) and then disappeared from the boat where she was supposedly being cared for and who also had something to do with a missing kitten or cat, had reached a point where she could no longer ignore the situation. Thus, she had come to the police station to ask for the assistance of DI Evans in identifying and locating the enigmatic child.

Chapter 23

'Child missing from Hartford, last seen in village of Potterton'

The headline emblazoned across the top of the Daily Messenger, drew the attention of most of the residents of Potterton and the surrounding villages. It wasn't often that the name of their modestly unassuming town hit the National or even the County newspapers and to feature so prominently was nothing if not extraordinary. The news was met with sadness by many readers; with anger from those who felt that not enough was done to keep our youngsters safe these days, and with determination to help find the missing child from those who had time and inclination to take part in a local search. There are often individuals who make it their business to pry into the misfortunes of others as well as some people who are looking for sensationalism and newsworthy items with which to boost their own careers. And, of course, there are the genuine ones who care deeply when tragedies strike strangers and who will give unstintingly of their time and efforts to try and find solutions in such circumstances.

Accordingly, local businesses stocked up on wellingtons, whistles, walking poles, warm socks, binoculars, torches and other items that might prove useful when searching for a missing child. The village tea shop baked extra cakes and pastries and

Nelly at the Pig and Whistle aired the several, largely unused, bedrooms in the expectation of many more visitors than usual.

It wasn't long before the influx began and DI Evans, who had called for extra back-up from Headquarters, led a team of specialist trackers and searchers to the town hall where he had set up an information and enquiry centre. Signs on all the main roads into Potterton directed visitors to the hall in an attempt to sensibly co-ordinate the various search parties.

Parking was proving to be a problem; the small central carpark was already overflowing before lunchtime and it was fortunate that the local farmer, whose land abutted the western limits of the town, kindly permitted extra parking in two of his meadows that were currently lying fallow.

By late afternoon about two hundred and fifty people, some local and many outsiders were scouring the town, working in ever-increasing circles outward from the town hall. The idea was to eliminate any chance of the girl being hidden in a house or garage, or even a garden shed or caravan before widening the search to include the riverbanks and countryside further afield.

A television camera crew had arrived and the national evening news included a five-minute item from the area.

DI Evans wasn't sure whether he was pleased or not. It would inevitably trigger even more visitors from afar and it would become more and more difficult to manage a controlled search with too many 'helpers'. The best he could hope for was that the girl would be found quickly and safely. If she was being held somewhere against her will, then perhaps all the media attention would frighten the captor into letting her go. If not, then perhaps a ransom note would appear and then, at least, they would have something more positive on which to base their searching. If she had already met with some dreadful accident (which didn't really bear considering) then hopefully a body might be found. Not the outcome he would wish for under any circumstances, but it would at least draw a line under the case and alter what the searchers were looking for.

***

Wilfred watched the goings on with growing dismay. When a ransom demand was mentioned (in the TV report, he thought) he physically shook and in the privacy of his own kitchen, firstly looked at the boarded-up window, and secondly pulled the crumpled paper from his pocket and read it again. The only comfort that he could take from its contents was that the threat to 'punish' Sophie, implied that she was alive. He looked again at the kitchen clock; he still had twenty minutes before he must leave the house.

He thought he knew the way to the old Mill but he also remembered that the track that led down to the river and on toward the Mill, hadn't been used in a long time and would be overgrown and difficult to follow. Nevertheless, he would take his garden knife and secateurs to cut away the worst of the brambles and the thought crossed his mind that the knife might also come in handy should he have the need to defend himself. Who knew what the sender of the note had in mind?

He nearly leapt out of his skin when he heard the back door open but his relief at seeing Steve enter the kitchen, compensated for any fright that he might have had to admit to.

"You didn't think I'd let you go alone, did you?" Steve attempted a brief smile but the frown lines that furrowed his brow bore witness to his concern. "Come on, it's going to take some time to get through the town with all these extra people about. They've called off the search for today and many have gone to the hotel in Hartford but there are still an awful lot of bodies crowding the Pig and Whistle as well as the Tea rooms that have stayed open for the evening."

***

Porkpie was sitting almost alone, in Kevin's cabin. The only other company was the still unnamed bird. Nameless because Kevin was anxious not to encourage it to be anything other than wild in order that it could survive once it was released back into nature. Nevertheless, it had become used to the few humans that came and went from time to time and was no longer afraid of the small cat which largely left it alone.

Kevin had already considered freeing it since it appeared to be fully recovered from whatever ailment had caused its earlier distress, but he was reluctant to do so without Sophie's presence. She and the bird had arrived together and he, unusually sentimental and subconsciously linking their stories with that of the little cat (also unnamed), felt that it wouldn't be right to release the one until he knew that the other was safe.

Porkpie (even she no longer thought of herself as Mary) found herself analysing the events of the last few days and, in particular, the conversation with DI Evans. On their arrival at the station, she and Kevin had been asked to wait whilst the Inspector dealt firstly with the smartly dressed lawyer who had an appointment and then with Wendy Crispin the social worker who also had other urgent business to attend to.

The waiting gave Kevin an opportunity to tell her in more detail what Beanie had discovered about the cameras. Apparently, they were linked to other security cameras placed in strategic positions throughout the town centre, all of which fed back to a central monitoring computer based at the Police headquarters in Hartford. The local station could also access the recordings, if necessary, by logging in to a specific server and by using security details which were known only to them.

The most relevant piece of information was that concerning the time scales where only five days' worth of filming was available at any one time. As far as the two of them were concerned, it was absolutely imperative that last Thursday's recording was looked at immediately before any potentially helpful footage was lost by overwriting.

When they eventually managed to see him, DI Evans had been extremely interested in what Porkpie and Kevin suggested and promised to access the video as soon as possible. He thanked them for reminding him of the CCTV cameras at the marina and he made notes on the squashy hatted person that Porkpie had observed in the Pig and Whistle. He couldn't promise to let them know what was recorded, since that was a private matter between the police and the owner of the marina. However, he assured them both, now that the missing child had become a police matter, that they could be certain that he, personally, would deal with the case and that their sleuthing had been very helpful, thank you.

"Very helpful, is that all?" Kevin had fumed on their way back to the marina. It was utterly infuriating how the police took everything into their own hands, more or less dismissing anything that an ordinary human being might be able to contribute. "Well, they're not going to get rid of me that easily!" he declared. And so it was that he, Kevin, would continue to search for Sophie, particularly within the marina, on the grounds that there were several boats and storage sheds that could easily accommodate a small child, and to which he had keys and thereby, access. She surely couldn't be too far away; after all, the abductor had carried her away from the boat and there had been no signs of a vehicle nearby. Time was of the essence and he, Kevin, was not going to stop looking for her until either she turned up of her own accord, or she was found; dead or alive.

Porkpie was to wait in the boat in case Sophie managed to find her way back. Niggling at the back of her mind was something that she had overheard when DI Evans had escorted the besuited lawyer out of the interview room and to the front door of the station.

"…make some further enquiries… births, deaths and marriages… blood relative… probate…" How could a lawyer be involved in the situation? Perhaps it had nothing to do with Sophie and it was simply coincidental that the lawyer had an appointment at that particular moment.

Gradually the exertions and anxieties of the last few days started to take their toll and Porkpie began to relax in the warmth of the cosy cabin. She leant her head back against the comfortable cushions and against her better judgement or her well founded intentions, her eyes began to close and she slept.

Chapter 24

Steve turned off the headlights of the rental car as he let it coast down the slight slope toward a rickety gate that bore a faded sign, "Langley's Mill, Potterton." There, below the words and almost illegible, was what remained of a telephone number, although Wilfred knew at once that it was no longer in use. Apart from the fact that most modern companies had resorted to using mobile phone technology, this number was only nine digits long and all national numbers now included an area code which resulted in them having approximately thirteen. All these thoughts shot through his mind at high speed and although he made a mental note of what he was seeing, none of it was important. The only thing that mattered was finding Sophie and, at the same time, avoiding any confrontation with the person who had requested his attendance here at this time.

In actual fact, they were earlier than anticipated. Having had a much easier journey through the town centre than Steve had predicted, they now had time to assess the situation. Since the note had demanded that Wilfred come alone, they agreed that Steve would take a slightly more circuitous route to the old building in order to avoid bumping into whoever it was that had sent the note. He parked the car a couple of hundred yards up the road and tucked into a gateway so as to be mainly out of sight before setting off through the undergrowth.

In the meantime, Wilfred would wait near the gate. The note had said come to the old Mill. It didn't specify where exactly and the track was sufficiently overgrown to make ingress difficult, if not impossible. Wilfred wondered how it had been possible to get a reluctant child through to the building; if indeed she was actually in the mill. Perhaps she wasn't in there at all and this had just been a convenient meeting place? Or perhaps she had been sedated and therefore not able to resist being taken anywhere. The possibilities were seemingly endless and Wilfred put his hands over his eyes as he tried to rub away all the dreadful scenarios that insisted on crowding into his mind.

He had only waited a short while when he heard footsteps approaching. He was about to turn to greet the newcomer when a hessian sack was thrown roughly over his head and he was knocked to the ground. His head hit the tarmac road surface hard and all went black.

**

Steve, working as quickly and quietly as he could, was cutting his way through the tangled undergrowth. Wilfred's secateurs were old and not as sharp as they might be, so the going was frustratingly slow. Nevertheless, he was relieved to hear water as it fell over a weir from the mill pond into a backwater and then out to re-join the main course of the river. At last, the building came into sight. Roofless and windowless, the only remaining evidence of its previous use was the gently rotting water-wheel. It must have been a magnificent sight in its hey-day; even now and despite the darkness, it was picturesque and atmospheric.

Steve worked his way round to where the front doors would have been and carefully listened; hoping to hear the cries of a child or any other noise that might indicate her presence. But there was nothing. He cautiously switched on his torch and shone it into the blackness. A rat or two scuttled away from the unexpected light, carefully skirting round the edges of what was once the floor and drawing Steve's attention to the fact that there was no floor remaining, no stairs to an upper level and no inner walls. The building was just a shell and probably exceedingly dangerous to enter. He hoped very much indeed that his daughter was not hidden away in this treacherous place.

He switched off the light and turned to look around him; hoping that he might see an alternative hiding place. It occurred to him then, just as Wilfred had wondered, that perhaps she wasn't here at all and the mill was a decoy or a convenient meeting place away from the town and prying eyes.

***

As he came to, Wilfred realised that he was in a moving vehicle. He hadn't heard a car engine before the sack was thrown over his head so he presumed that he must have been unconscious long enough for his captor to fetch some form of transport to him and to manhandle him into the back of whatever it was. A van maybe? Or he could be in the boot of a car, but since it was dark and his hands were tied and his head still covered, he had no way of knowing where he was. He lay still and listened but no one spoke and apart from the gentle hum of the vehicle's engine, all was silent.

***

Steve swore softly to himself as yet another bramble dug through his trousers and into his leg, ripping the skin so that he could feel a trickle of blood as it ran down to his sock. He was sorely tempted to turn back since the impenetrable wall of tangled briars barred his way. However, as he looked back over his shoulder, he realised that even that idea offered no easier option and for a moment or two he regretted even beginning this impossible adventure.

Adventure? No! That made it seem as though he'd had a choice in the matter but this was his daughter for whom he was searching and hadn't he abandoned her enough times already? He would have to do much more than simply find her to put right the wrongs he had perpetrated throughout her short life. She hadn't deserved the unkindness he had inflicted upon her; shutting her away in her room while he and her mother argued vociferously and vitriolically about things of which she, at such a tender age, should have had no understanding.

With no real thought for his daughter, he had walked out on her, his wife and their unborn child. Cowardice and a lack of trust between husband and wife was what caused the rift, and immaturity, selfishness and stubbornness is what prevented him returning to put things right until it was too late. When he heard that his wife, Julie, had found a new partner, Steve had been far away on the other side of the world and enjoying a bachelor existence in Australia. It was all too easy to forget about his responsibilities; his children. He had never even met his son; a sob escaped him as he stood surrounded by the tangled foliage and acknowledged to himself that he had similarly entangled his life before the son he'd never known had lost his. And now with Julie having taken her own life, he wasn't about to lose his daughter as well. "No!" he whispered, "No!" he said, "NO!" he shouted.

The answering cry was faint. He stood stock still and listened, trying to determine where the sound had come from. He called again, "Hello," and the answering, muffled, "help me," came from lower down the gently sloping hillside. In his haste to get to the source of the cry, Steve rushed forward but his leg was caught in the grip of brambles and he fell heavily onto his stomach. He dropped the torch and the secateurs as he slid out from under the bushes, ripping his trousers to shreds as he fell and coming to a halt against a low brick wall that had once been part of a landing stage for the barges that came to take the flour away from the old mill.

To his right was a still standing building that had once served as an office for the boatmen. It was barely recognisable since it was largely overgrown by ivy and what remained of any windows were boarded over, but Steve remembered coming here as a boy with his pals from school. They had always approached it from the river using whichever floating device they could beg, borrow or steal from the marina. This was where he had tried his first cigarette and where he had first kissed a girl. The memories came flooding back as he scrambled to his feet intending to find the source of the cry for help.

He immediately crouched back down and once more scuttled behind the wall. Struggling toward the building from the far side of where Steve was hiding, but just about visible if he leaned carefully around the end of the wall, was a dark figure whose silhouette in the pale moonlight showed a squashy hat. Dragged behind the shapeless hatted being was another bound and head-covered individual that was obviously struggling and doing its best to avoid being taken to where it very clearly did not want to go. Ineffective in its struggle, it was shoved through an opened door and disappeared from Steve's line of sight.

The first man stood up straight and brushed his hands together as if to indicate a job well done. He closed the door and fiddled with a lock of some sort before making his way back to wherever he had come from. However, not before Steve had managed to get a good look at the man, the hat and the direction he took. He waited until he was quite sure that the coast was clear before quietly making his way across the small yard and tapping gently on the now locked door.

Chapter 25

Kevin knew the marina like the back of his hand. Had you asked him how long he had lived and worked there, he would not have been able to tell you the precise number of years. His usual answer to such enquiries would be a shrug and, "How long is a piece of string?" When you looked at him, head on one side in puzzlement, he would grin and say, "Doesn't matter provided it's long enough!"

"Long enough for what?" you ask again.

"Long enough to do whatever you want it to do!"

It wasn't that he was trying to be obtuse, it was simply that time didn't matter to him; if there was work to be done and he was there to do it, then do it he would. It was precisely this attitude that made him popular and considered trustworthy by the owners of the marina, the hire companies and the people to whom the various long-term moorings were leased. He had in his possession keys to almost all of the boats and sheds that were to be found there on that particular evening and so, having tapped on the sides of sheds and roofs of cabins, he opened each door and boarded each craft to look carefully in all of the places that a young child might hide.

He wasn't surprised to find so few people about. Not all the boats were occupied at this time of year and the town was an exciting place to be that evening, so any youngsters had almost certainly gone there to join in the fun. The few older people welcomed him aboard, offered him cups of tea or coffee, and fully understood when, after explaining his mission on this occasion, he refused their offerings. They all wished him well and hoped he would find the girl soon.

There was only one boat to which he did not have keys. It was moored at the far end of the last staithe, on the left of the main yard and on the opposite side of the river from Kevin's boat. It was not a regular visitor and when he knocked on the cabin door, he was answered by the frantic yapping of what was almost certainly a small, terrier type dog. He knocked again and leant round the side of the cockpit to peer through a cabin window which was ajar; presumably to allow ventilation for the dog left inside.

Since it was fairly late, dark and the bared teeth of the small, white dog made it perfectly clear that he would not be welcomed in should he attempt to force the door, he decided that he would call it a night and make his way back to his own boat. He would come here again first thing in the morning and hope to find someone aboard. Despite his instincts telling him that he would not find Sophie nearby, he couldn't help feeling tired and disappointed that his search had revealed absolutely nothing helpful.

When he eventually made his way back to his home, he was surprised, firstly to discover lights on, secondly by the small grey cat that shot out from the opened door and disappeared up onto the bank, and thirdly by the sleeping form of Porkpie who was curled on his sofa, hat still on her head and snoring gently.

An unexpected feeling of pleasure brought a smile to his face as he fetched a blanket from the bedchamber and tucked it carefully around the somnolent form. She stirred a little and murmured in her sleep, "Night, night dear." And he, in response and without forethought, bent down and kissed her lightly on her forehead. "Sleep well."

***

Beanie had not been able to sleep. She had made herself her customary mug of cocoa, showered and changed into her nightgown and had even got into bed and picked up the book she had been trying to read. However, her mind was racing and the words would not stay in the right order to make any sort of sense so she put the book down, sat up and reached for her fleecy dressing gown. She slipped her feet into her slippers and made her way back into the kitchen. Perhaps she needed something a little stronger to help her sleep.

There was a bottle of brandy somewhere at the back of one of these cupboards. Neither she nor her sister were regular drinkers; wine for a birthday or Christmas occasion and a medicinal brandy for coughs and colds. She wasn't surprised to find the bottle more than half empty since she had no idea when they had bought it or how long it had resided in the cupboard. She found a glass and poured herself a couple of fingers. "I think that's how they measure it," she muttered, "anyway, it'll have to do."

She sipped it carefully and, finding it rather nice, poured herself a little more while she worried about where on earth her sister could be. It was most unlike her not to be home in time for supper although she could understand that on this occasion there was much else to think about.

She took another slurp from the now half-empty glass, topped it up from the bottle and began to wonder whether there was more than meets the eye to Mary's recent obsession with Kevin and his boat. She seemed to spend an awful lot of time there these days. She took another swig from the glass and then, as she attempted to plonk it unsteadily on the kitchen counter, it fell to the tiled floor and smashed. "Good job it was empty again!" she thought and then, "Why do they make these glasses so small?" Never mind, she would drink the rest straight from the bottle; that ought to do the trick and get her off to sleep.

Just as she put the bottle to her lips and tipped her head back to drain the last few drops muttering, "Waste not, want not," there was an almighty crashing noise right outside her kitchen window. It was followed by the yowl of a cat and the yelp of a small dog.

Her senses dulled by the unusual quantity of alcohol she had imbibed, Beanie turned to look out of the window, just in time to see a white shape disappear down the towpath, away from the marina.

"Goodness! What on earth was that?" she asked of no one, since there was no one present to ask, "I'd better go and see what's what!" Clumsily she took off her dressing-gown and slippers. She pulled on her old grey mackintosh and pushed her feet into the wrong wellington boots. She wondered why they didn't seem to fit properly as she staggered down the garden path, through the gate and out onto the towpath.

About fifty yards beyond the sisters' cabin, the channel curved to the left before joining the main course of the river just beyond a footbridge. The bridge marked the end of the marina access and there was no further path on that side of the river. The towpath on the righthand side followed the curve of the bank before disappearing into a wooded area just beyond, which was the opening to a mill stream and an associated pool, weir and mill race. There were some old buildings on that side which, she knew, were only accessible from a very overgrown track leading down from a now almost disused back lane.

As Beanie made her way very unsteadily down the towpath, she looked to the left and saw what she thought was a little ghost racing skilfully across the parapet of the footbridge. At the same moment she heard a splosh, followed by another yelp and then further frantic splashing. It took her more than a minute or two to make sense of what she was witnessing but one thing was certain; something was in the water, something needed help and the bank was much too high for such a small something to climb out unaided.

"A boat," she muttered, "I need a boat." She turned and made her way, a little less unsteadily, back towards the cabin. Her wrong booted feet made walking quickly rather difficult and she waddled to the bottom of her garden where there was an old boatshed. "I'm sure there used to be a boat in here," as she yanked open a rotting door and, "Yesss!" she hissed as she found the equally rotten dinghy. Taking the oars from where they were propped against a wall, she heaved and tugged with alcohol fuelled strength to get the boat down the overgrown slipway and into the water.

By the time she had succeeded, one boot was full of water and the hem of her nightgown, which hung below the bottom of her mackintosh, had snagged on brambles and goosegrass as she forced her way down the bank. "At last," she breathed as she clambered aboard, sat on the mid-thwart and placed the oars in their rowlocks.

It was a long time since she had rowed a dinghy. In fact, it was so long ago that she could barely remember how it was done. However, similar to riding a bicycle, once you've mastered the skill, you never completely forget. Her progress was erratic to say the least; she found herself in the reeds by the bank, firstly on the left side and then on the right. "Why didn't someone develop a way of rowing so that you can see where you're going?" she opined as she pushed herself away from the bank once again.

At last, she found a rhythm; in, pull, out, back, in, pull... she was making reasonable progress toward the still splashing object. What she hadn't noticed was the amount of water inside the boat. Gradually, it covered her feet, then it seeped into her wellingtons and before she had reached her destination she was sitting in water.

Suddenly the small, struggling white object was right under her left blade. She immediately dropped both oars and lurched wildly to grab whatever it was. Naturally right-handed, she had reached across her own body to take hold of the object. By doing so she unbalanced the already sinking craft so that the gunwale dipped below the surface, further flooding the little boat, which promptly sank, depositing her and everything else into the river. Spluttering and gasping, but determined not to lose hold of her 'treasure' she splashed her way to the nearest bank which just happened to be the side without a towpath.

Chapter 26

Sopping wet, dazed and beginning to shiver, Beanie clutched the equally wet and shaking dog to her ample bosom. The prospect of entering the water once more in order to get to the towpath and home, was too much to bear. The way to the footbridge on her right was barred by a thick hedge and a barbed wire fence and to the left were a forest of stinging nettles and brambles. What was she to do? She undoubtedly couldn't stay where she was for much longer since she had already almost certainly caught a chill which could rapidly become pneumonia if she wasn't able to get dry and warm soon.

The truth was that there really wasn't an alternative option so, taking a deep breath as she made up her mind to brave the waters once more, she began to scramble to her feet. At that point the same small grey ghost she had earlier perceived running daintily across the top rail of the footbridge, dashed past her feet and into the vegetation behind her. Immediately the soggy doggy leapt out of her arms and chased after the cat.

"Ungrateful wretch!" Beanie wondered how she had let the creature lead her into this predicament, "Now what to do?" The numbing effects of a fairly large dose of brandy had begun to wear off and Beanie was able to look around more carefully to see exactly where the two animals had gone. Behind her was a very small gap in the undergrowth, "A game trail is what Mary would have called it," where badgers or muntjac deer came to the water to drink. Beanie knelt down on all fours and crawled carefully through the tiny tunnel.

***

Steve knocked again and called out softly, "Anyone in there? Can you hear me?" and then waited, listening for the response which did not come. Uncertain as to how far away the squashy hatted man had gone, he was wary of making too much noise. He worked his way carefully round what was left of the building only to find that it was largely a shell of roof, some outer walls and a concrete floor. It wasn't large but was built into a bank that sloped steeply up and away from the water. It was only as he was making his way back to the door at one end that he noticed a very small barred window at ground level.

Although there was no light behind the window which was obviously boarded up on the inside, there were a few cracks between the panels and he shone his torchlight in, hoping he might illuminate something helpful. He could determine that there was some sort of chamber below the upper floor level but it really couldn't have been very large and had perhaps been used as a store room for ropes and other boating paraphernalia. With a lurch of his heart, he realised that it probably was big enough to hide a small girl and perhaps an elderly man too.

As he made his way back to the still locked door, he was startled by the sudden appearance of a little grey cat which skidded to a halt right by his feet and closely followed by a slightly larger, bedraggled looking dog. Abruptly as the chase ended; the dog sat down and the cat began to scrabble at the bottom of the door.

Astonished, Steve looked from one to the other and scratched his head. At that moment a third apparition appeared from under the greenery. It groaned once or twice before scrambling to its feet and brushing ineffectually at the various bits of detritus that had attached themselves to her dripping clothes. One wellington had disappeared completely and the other squelched wetly as the figure staggered towards him and held out a hand, "Good evening," it spoke, "I wonder if you could help me?"

The incongruity of the situation struck Steve as incredibly funny and, despite his worry and concern for his missing daughter and her step-grandfather, found himself laughing aloud. The woman, for female she was, judging by her soaked and tatty attire, was affronted in the extreme, "Well, if that's the best you can manage, then I'm sorry I asked you. Goodbye!" The last of the alcohol in her system provided her with false bravado and Beanie drew herself up as proudly as her current condition would allow and made to walk away, up the overgrown driveway.

"Stop!" Steve called her back, "Look, I'm sorry, this whole situation is quite ridiculous, but I shouldn't have laughed. The truth is I might just as easily have cried." Quickly and as briefly as possible he explained who he was and what he was doing there; "...and so you see, I think they must both be in there." and he pointed to the locked door where the little cat was still trying to claw its way through the rotting wood.

***

Sophie had been asleep when the door was wrenched open. She sat up, startled by both the sound and the unexpected light, albeit moonlight, that invaded the small cellar. Before she had a chance to speak; to call out and ask for help, something large and awkward fell down the stairs towards her and landed in her lap, causing her to fall backwards against the hard wall. All went black.

She had no idea how long she had been unconscious. It could have been minutes, hours or even days, but she opened her eyes to see a half-recognised face leaning anxiously over her. For a moment she was confused and thought perhaps she was dreaming, "Uncle Wilfred? What are you doing here? Where's Mummy?" and a sob as she remembered where she was. Then, in a rush, as is often the case with pent-up emotion and no proper outlet, "I want to go home. I'm sorry I ran away but I want my Mum now and I'll be good for her so long as she doesn't send me away to live with someone else."

Wilfred shook his head sadly and a tear rolled down his cheek. The duct tape over his mouth made it impossible to answer the girl and his hands were tied behind his back with cable ties. He needed her to help him before he could help her but she was too young and too wrapped up in her own misery to see or comprehend his need.

It was then that he heard the tap on the door and the familiar voice calling him softly. Sophie sobbed quietly with her face buried in her hands. It was pitch black and neither of them could see anything save for the whites of each other's eyes. He couldn't reply. Steve would go away and he and the girl would be stuck here for ever. They would die…

Suddenly, he had an idea. Unable to see exactly where she was, he lashed out with his foot and kicked the girl hard on what happened to be her shin. She cried out, "OUCH!" – just what he intended. He kicked again and she shrieked in terror, "AAGHH! Stop it. That hurts!"

He wanted to put his arms around her, to reassure her, to explain why he had hurt her; but he could do nothing but wait…

***

163

"I think I should get you home," Steve was worried for the well-being of this extremely damp lady. He didn't really want to leave this place until he had ascertained that neither Wilfred nor Sophie was behind that door. The little cat would not leave and ran from door to boarded window and back, scrabbling and mewing at both. The dog had submitted to being leashed with a piece of twine that had been lying on the ground and both he and the woman shivered almost uncontrollably.

"Come on, my car is a little way up the lane, I'll take you and then come back."

He had just finished speaking when a yell came from behind the door; "OUCH," was muffled but instantly recognisable as a cry of pain.

"My God, she's in there!"

"Oh, my Lord, that's Sophie!" both spoke at once and pushing the cat to one side, Steve began to wrestle with the door.

The wood was old although the lock was strong, but the hinges were the first to give way. Mindless of damage to fingernails or skin, both Steve and Beanie worked together to destroy the ancient door. At last, it was open enough for Steve to shine his torch down the creaky wooden staircase and into the upturned faces of Wilfred and Sophie.

He would never forget the look of pure terror in Sophie's eyes or the mixture of relief and despair in Wilfred's.

Chapter 27

It was a very odd-looking group of people that stood on the bank outside Kevin's boat and a very surprised couple who appeared sleepily in response to the insistent knocking.

As soon as he stepped out of the cabin and up into the cockpit well, Sophie dropped the cat and flung herself into Kevin's arms. The cat ran inside and onto Sophie's bed where it washed itself thoroughly before curling up and falling into a deep sleep.

Porkpie looked curiously at the figure that appeared to be her sister but what on earth was she doing out here, at this time of night and in an almost unrecognisable state of dishevelment; wearing goodness knew what, with only one boot and with twigs and leaves adorning her bare head. "Beanie?" she asked hesitantly, at which the shorter, plumper, usually self-assured woman promptly burst into tears. Grabbing a warm coat from just inside the door, Porkpie almost leapt up onto the bank and wrapped her sobbing sister in both the coat and her arms.

As she began to usher the weeping woman down the towpath toward their home, she turned and looked curiously at the two men who still stood next to the gangplank. "Are you both alright?" she asked, "you can come back with me if you like." But the younger man shook his head, "No, thank you," he replied, "I'll take Wilfred home now. I'm sure you want to know what has been happening so I'll come back a bit later on and fill you in and I need to find out where this rascal belongs too," he looked down at the grubby little dog still leashed with a piece of string.

As she turned away to continue homeward, he added, "Thanks for looking after Sophie. I'll sort something out for her as soon as I can."

"And who might you be?" All sorts of alarm bells rang in Porkpie's head as she faced the thought of losing the child yet again.

"I'm her father," he said.

***

DI Evans was both relieved and pleasantly surprised to receive the news early that morning. He hadn't relished the thought of a prolonged public search and all the media attention that such activities attracted. Whilst appreciating that the small town would probably benefit from the extra visitors, it certainly didn't make policing the area any easier.

He would let Wendy Crispin know the good news; that the missing child was no longer missing and she would ensure that suitable arrangements were made for her continuing care. There was, of course, the slight issue of informing Dave Clarkson, formally known as David Clarke, that he had no parental rights over Sophie and nor was he in line to inherit the Martin's house, but he felt confident that he could leave that to Paul Wood, the solicitor dealing with Mrs Martin's probate. On the other hand, he must be certain that Steve Clarkson was indeed the biological and legal parent of the young girl; not that he had any real doubts, but there were processes, for example, DNA testing, to be followed in cases such as this.

The one mystery that remained unresolved was the abduction of Sophie from Kevin Parker's boat. The only piece of evidence that he had regarding that part of this case was a scruffy scrap of paper which, he had been assured, was thrown through a window at the home of Sophie's grandparents in Meadow Walk. He had no doubt at all that Wilfred Martin was telling the truth. He had no reason whatsoever to lie and the broken window bore evidence after the fact. Wilfred had been too upset to speak to him earlier and so the only information he had on that front came from Steve Clarkson who had spoken on his behalf.

He made a mental note to interview Wilfred in person later on and to follow up on Steve's story about living abroad for the past couple of years.

Of course, there had also been the somewhat vague description of a person wearing a squashy hat who, it was claimed, had been responsible for Wilfred's capture and subsequent imprisonment at the old Mill complex. Perhaps this same person had been Sophie's abductor – but who was he and what was his motivation? Was he working alone or was he in the employ of someone else?

**

"Well, you properly buggered that up didn't you, you silly old idiot!" Dave was fuming at the incompetence of this man who claimed to be an expert. He couldn't express himself as strongly as he would have liked since they were in a rather exposed position in the overfull Pig and Whistle which was more usually pretty quiet and empty at this time of day.

Opposite him, the squashy hatted figure hunched his shoulders so that his head almost disappeared into the upturned collar of his overcoat. "How was I to know he had someone with him?" he opined.

"It was your job to know! Don't think I'm going to pay you now. All that explosive was expensive and all for nothing; you bloody moron."

Unbeknownst to Squashy hat, much later that night, Dave had gone to the old mill intending to throw some grenades down into the storage chamber; thereby disposing of both Wilfred and Sophie, and thus clearing the way for him to inherit the house in Meadow Walk. On finding the door smashed open and the two incumbents gone, he had sworn and fumed and stamped like a thwarted child before carrying his ire back to throw at Squashy hat who had been expecting to meet him to receive payment for his services.

Accepting that he definitely would not obtain any further monies and not wanting to risk personal damage or further abuse from this employer, Squashy hat rose swiftly from his seat and scuttled out of the door. Had you been watching him, you might have seen him take the recognisable hat from his head and stuff it into a municipal waste bin.

***

True to his word, Wilfred welcomed DI Evans into his kitchen and showed him the boarded-up window and the brick around which the note had been tied. He explained how he and Steve, whom he had recognised as his late step-daughter's husband, had gone to the mill as the note requested. The only deviation being that they went together and not Wilfred alone as the note had demanded. The rest Evans already knew and he left a little later, feeling confident that the only remaining mystery was the identity of the perpetrator of and the reasons for the double abduction. It seemed reasonable to assume that Dave Clarkson was somehow behind the whole affair; especially in view of his keenness to ascertain his right to inherit Mrs Martin's house.

***

Monday morning, Dave was waiting impatiently on Paul Woods' office doorstep. As soon as the door was opened by a smiling Helen, he pushed past her demanding to see Paul immediately.

Helen kept her proficient cool and asked him to sit whilst she informed Mr Woods of his presence. Despite his irritation at being kept waiting, Dave did as he was asked, but his leg jigged up and down as his fingers tapped on the low coffee table.

"Can I get you a coffee? Mr Woods will be with you shortly. He's just dealing with another urgent matter. Sorry to keep you waiting." Ever professional, Helen knew she was playing for time. She sat at her desk on the other side of the small waiting room and shuffled various papers and documents until a buzzer sounded and, "You can go in now," she said.

The enforced wait had only served to make Dave even more anxious to get this business over. The sooner he had the signed confirmation of ownership in his hands, the better. However, it wasn't long before raised voices emanated from the back office and the sound of a falling chair suggested that someone had stood up abruptly. At that precise moment, DI Evans came in through the external door.

"Thank goodness, you're just in time!" Helen was mightily relieved.

"What do you mean, it's not mine?" Dave's roar could have been heard several blocks away,

"We'll see about that!" he threatened as the inner door burst open and the angry man reappeared in the waiting area. He came to an abrupt halt as DI Evans held up his police identity badge and said, "Mr Dave Clarkson?" Without waiting for a reply, he continued, "I'm arresting you on suspicion of fraud, impersonation and abduction of a minor with intent to cause bodily harm." He recited legal warnings as he fastened handcuffs around the man's wrists and led him out to a waiting police car.

Chapter 28

Tilda jumped up and down in excitement. "Really?" she asked, "She's really coming to live here with me?" and without waiting for an answer, "When? When is she coming?"

"After school today!" Carol laughed at the young girl's pleasure, "You can walk home together and I'll have tea ready and waiting for you both."

Carol had been surprised and pleased to hear from Wendy Crispin and doubly so when she heard her request. Of course, she'd be delighted to have Sophie come and stay for a few weeks; perhaps until the end of the summer term. Her father, Steve, needed to return to Canada to tie up some loose ends before looking for work over here. He hoped that he would be able to stay in this area and was keen for Sophie to be with friends, starting with someone she already knew. Tilda fitted the bill exactly and Sophie had been almost as excited as her friend to know that they would not only go to school together but could live in the same house.

At first Carol had been a little dubious about taking in the sister of little Alfie; she would never be able to forget her devastation at that disastrous time but, when she thought about it, perhaps this was her opportunity to try to make amends. Maybe she could do for the girl what she hadn't been able to do for her little brother. It was doubly tragic that Sophie's mother had also taken her own life, as well as the grandmother coming to an unfortunate end. How could one small person cope with so many losses in such a short time?

Thank goodness Steve had reappeared. He was a good man whom Carol had always liked. They had been at the same school as teenagers, although in different year groups. It wouldn't be difficult working with him to help Sophie find her feet and those new friends of hers; the people at the marina? Well, they may be a bit odd but they were certainly kind and caring and Sophie had found refuge and comfort there when everything else around her had gone topsy turvy.

***

Sophie's only acknowledged concern, which she voiced as she and Porkpie were packing up her few belongings ready to take to her new home, was that she didn't want to lose her new friends at the marina. Aunty Pie, Uncle Kev and Auntie Bea had become very important to her and together they represented the first real stability that she'd experienced in her short life.

"You won't lose us," Aunty Pie had assured, "you can come to visit any time when you're not in school and you can bring Tilda with you too if she'd like to come."

"I'll make her want to come!" Sophie declared happily before a worried frown creased her brow. "What about the cat and the bird? Can they

173

come with me?" she asked. Porkpie shook her head, "I don't think that would be a good idea. They are happy here; at least the cat is, the bird I'm not so sure. I think it might be time to let it go back to its own kind. What do you think?"

"I suppose…" she looked doubtful and thoughtful as Kevin came into the cabin. "What's up?" he asked. Porkpie smiled at him and explained the conundrum.

"Well, as it happens, I was going to suggest that we take the bird back to where I found him to let him go free, right now!"

"Oh…" Sophie looked doubtful, since she had become very attached to her animal friends, and then, hesitantly, "alright, if you're sure he'll be safe?"

"I'll keep an eye on him," Kevin assured her as he rummaged under the bed and pulled out an old birdcage. "He can travel in this!"

Soon all three of them and the birdcage were crammed into the cab of Kevin's old pickup truck. He drove carefully, away from the town of Potterton for about half an hour before coming to a halt at the side of a country lane on the edge of Hingemont, a nearby hamlet.

A flock of rooks were feeding on insects and young shoots from the field, but they flew up as one and landed in some nearby trees where plenty of nests showed that it was their home. The vehicle stopped and the occupants scrambled out. Kevin carried the cage a little way into the hedgeless field and set it down on the ground before opening wide the door.

The bird hopped to the exit and stood for a moment, its head on one side. Then it stepped out of the cage and paused again before looking directly up at Kevin as if to say, "Thanks, mate." It cawed once and then spread its wings and flapped as it flew gracefully up into the sky. It circled low over the truck and dipped its head at Sophie and Porkpie who stood behind her with her hands on the girl's shoulders. "Goodbye bird," Sophie whispered as it flew, across the field, away from the rookery and into the top of a lone tree that stood on the far side of the field.

Sophie clapped her hands and laughed delightedly, "A Single Rook!" she giggled as she clambered back into the truck.

Later, as Sophie climbed into her bed for the last time aboard Kevin's boat, she hugged Kevin harder than usual and said, "Don't forget about me."

"As if I could," came the response, "and don't you forget about us!"

"As if I could," she giggled and then, "OH!" as her feet came into contact with a furry creature hiding under her bedclothes. The little grey cat, instead of leaping down and asking to be let out for its usual night of hunting, wound itself about Sophie's head, purring loudly.

"There is one thing you have forgotten," Porkpie had walked up quietly behind Kevin.

"What's that?"

"You still haven't given this little thing a name!"

Sophie stroked the beautiful cat's silky grey fur and thought for a moment or two, "Shadow," she said, "I'll call her Shadow, because she follows me, she's my shadow and she found me when I was lost. Look after her for me please?"

"Of course," both adults spoke in unison and their eyes met in mutual agreement.

"Sleep well Sophie, you have another new beginning tomorrow!"

Chapter 29

It had taken Beanie rather longer than she would have liked to recover from her evening of high jinks and excitement. Her impromptu wetting together with the rather large amount of brandy she had imbibed served to give her a serious chill which threatened to become pneumonia, as she had predicted. Fortunately, the quick actions of her caring sister, who had insisted on a hot bath, a hot drink and bed rest for twenty-four hours despite it being almost three o'clock in the morning when they arrived back at the cabin, had averted a total catastrophe. Beanie had slept for almost thirty-six hours and it was Sunday afternoon by the time she was up and dressed again.

During her unconscious hours, Porkpie had discovered; firstly, the empty brandy bottle, secondly, a smashed flower-pot which had undoubtedly been knocked off the windowsill during the cat and dog chase and thirdly, the opened boat shed and missing boat. Thus, by the time Beanie had awoken, there was very little explaining to be done apart from the bit that took place at the old mill. Fortunately, Steve and Wilfred had returned as promised and they were able to furnish Kevin and Porkpie with the rest of the story of how they had found and rescued Sophie.

The only puzzle that remained was that of the dog. Steve had taken it to Wilfred's home, bathed it and fed it from a tin of tuna that he found in Wilfred's cupboard. It looked to be a completely different dog that he brought back on a borrowed lead the following day. It was most definitely a small, white, male Jack Russell Terrier and as soon as it barred its teeth at Kevin, he knew exactly where he had seen it before! The last boat! The one he couldn't enter since he had no keys. A window had been left ajar to give the dog some air, but what the owners had apparently failed to note is that the dog was small enough and clever enough to climb out of the window. Especially when something as compulsive as a cat dared to show itself on the staithe to which the boat was moored!

The absence of the dog had been duly noted at the marina office so that when Kevin went to make enquiries, all was clear and the small canine was soon reunited with its owners. All is well that ends well as far as the dog was concerned. However, Kevin was thanked profusely by the couple who insisted on inviting him aboard for a cup of coffee. During his visit they chatted about their experiences in the Pig and Whistle and they described some of the other customers. He wasn't particularly interested and was only half listening and nodding, hopefully in the right places, when the husband mentioned something that made him sit up and take notice.

"It was his hat that took my eye! Never seen anything quite like it before. Sort of almost like an army hat but it was the squashiest thing I've ever seen. I probably wouldn't have taken much notice of it but the wearer was arguing with another, younger man. They were really at loggerheads until Squashy hat stood up and walked out! The other bloke was pretty fed up about something but I wasn't going to get involved! You certainly meet some peculiar people out here in the sticks!"

***

Porkpie knew that she was going to miss little Sophie. More than that, she knew she had enjoyed working closely with Kevin to provide and care for the little girl as well as the animals that had arrived concurrently. She supposed that now things would return to their former humdrum existence, although hopefully occasionally lifted by visits from Sophie and, perhaps, her friend.

Porkpie had arranged to take Sophie's belongings to Carol's house during day time and while the children were in school. Thus, she arrived mid-morning, as previously suggested, and the two women sat sipping coffee while Porkpie told Carol as much as she knew about Sophie's past and of the few days that she had stayed on the boat.

Was it really only a few days? It seemed so much longer; long enough to have formed a deep connection to the child and, she secretly admitted to herself, with Kevin. Brushing that thought aside, to ponder on later when she was alone with her thoughts, she explained to Carol how Sophie had been reluctant to talk about her past or explain why she had run away from home but that it was clear from her behaviours that she hadn't always been treated kindly. Carol was able to reassure the older lady that she knew a little more of Sophie's background although she couldn't quite bring herself to tell Mary the whole story.

Even the thought of little Alfie brought a lump to her throat and a tear to her eye. She couldn't mention his name, but she was able to demonstrate that she understood why Sophie had run away; that she was afraid of the same thing happening to her as had happened to her brother. Consequently, it was really important for Sophie to feel secure and loved which she most certainly was by all those whose paths she had crossed.

The one part that Sophie had not so far come to terms with was the death of her mother. Several times she had asked where she was and when would she be able to see her mum again. Vague responses had sufficed so far since there was much to distract a young mind from that particular issue. It had been agreed that at an appropriate opportunity and as soon as possible, the adults closest to Sophie would come together to support her in accepting the sad truth of her mother's demise. Above all, it was imperative that her father be involved in that activity and in the meantime, she would simply be allowed to believe that her mother was unwell and couldn't see her just now. As only a child can, Sophie accepted what she was told and didn't dwell on her mother's absence. Perhaps, in her heart, she already knew the truth?

Wendy Crispin had informed Carol of Sophie's step-grandfather who still resided in Meadow Walk and who would like to be a part of Sophie's life once he had got his own affairs sorted and in order. There had been alcohol involved, she understood, and it wouldn't do for Sophie to witness any further unpleasantness that might occur as a result of a slip-up in Wilfred's rehabilitation. Nevertheless, Steve, Sophie's father, planned to be living with Wilfred for a while once he returned from Canada and there was always the possibility of a reconciliation between the girl and her late Granny Milly's husband whom she knew as Uncle Wilfred.

"Ah, yes, Steve," Porkpie smiled, "I've met him and Wilfred," she wasn't about to elucidate the circumstance of their meeting but explained, "We've spent a little time together and we know their connection with Sophie. We'll be very happy to support any interaction between Sophie and her family. Perhaps you could all come and we'll share a picnic or something at the marina."

"That would be lovely," Carol felt happier than she had for a long time. New children to care for, new friends to support her and the children and, she realised, not just a new start for Sophie, but for her as well.

Chapter 30

It was a mild May evening and Kevin sat in the bow-end well of his narrow boat enjoying a final coffee before retiring for the night. It had been a long working week; Saturday always being the busiest since the hire-boat change-overs usually took place then as well as the owner-holiday makers who often ended their jaunts at the weekend, leaving Sunday to prepare themselves for a return to the work-place. Boats had to be cleaned, checked for damage, repaired when necessary and recharged, refilled and generally prepared for their next occupants and outings.

Consequently, having had very little time to think of anything other than work and deliberately not wondering or worrying about the girl to whom he had become unusually attached and whom he hardly dared admit he missed inordinately, he found himself aching for knowledge of how she fared.

He saw Mary approach before he heard her softly humming as she strode purposefully along the towpath. He smiled to himself and his heart lurched as he realised that it wasn't only Sophie that he had missed these past few days.

Porkpie didn't notice him sitting quietly and contemplatively at the forrard end of his home, but she tapped tentatively on the roof of the cabin before stepping down into the cockpit well.

"Come on through," Kevin called, as his head appeared above the long roof and he waved to her.

***

Earlier that same day, Beanie had accosted her sister as she stomped back into the kitchen and banged about making herself a pot of tea.

"Where have you been, Mary?" Beatrice only used her sister's given name when she had something of importance to say. Before Porkpie had a chance to respond, she answered herself saying, "Tramping about in those muddy fields I suppose and now you're trampling it all into my clean kitchen! I don't know what you find so interesting out there. Anyway, I want to talk to you."

"Our kitchen," Porkpie muttered as she carried the tea tray into the more comfortable sitting area and began to pour two cups of the brew. "Here," she said as she handed one to her sister, "What do you want to talk about?"

"You," retorted Beanie. Porkpie looked up in surprise. She had been expecting some snippet of gossip that Bea had picked up at her Sip and Sew meeting, or an interesting item of news from the paper she read each day but, "Me!?" she said in astonishment, "Why?"

"Well, you've been moping about with a long face all week. You don't speak to me and you don't tell me where you're going or when you're coming back. It was bad enough last week when you spent

183

all your time with that girl on the boat but at least then I knew where you were. Now I have no idea where you're going, what you're doing or even what you are thinking about. Yesterday was the last straw; you went out at the crack of dawn and you didn't come back until after I had gone to bed. Then you were out again before breakfast today. It's not good enough and it's not fair of you to leave me in the dark. On top of that, you're not even eating properly, so, I want to know what's going on with you?"

Much to her amazement, Porkpie slumped back in the chair she was perching on and breathed out like a deflating balloon. After a moment or two of sitting slouched with her eyes closed and her tea-cup dangerously close to spilling itself from her loosely held hand, she sighed again and whispered, "I miss her."

"Miss who... oh," Beanie understood at last. She stood up and took Porkpie's cup, placing it more safely on its saucer on the tray. Then she put her arms around her sister and waited for her to regain her usual composure.

After a few moments, a couple of hiccoughs and an occasional sniff, Porkpie pulled away from Beanie's embrace, "Thanks, Bea," she said, and then, "the truth is I miss him too!"

It was Beanie's turn to look incredulous. Her sister, pining for a man? Good gracious, it had been years and years since either of them had shown the slightest inkling of interest the opposite sex. They had long ago come to the conclusion that romance and marriage was not for them and they were content with their lot and with each other – or so she had thought…

She sat down abruptly in the opposite chair and stared at her sister's sorrowful face. After a few minutes silence, "You're… you're not… not in love, are you?" she hesitantly enquired.

"I don't know," that was the reality of it for Mary, "I don't think so," she continued, "but there was something so nice and ordinary and yet special about the two of us working together, looking after a little girl, a cat and a bird. I think it must have been a bit like having a family of my own. It's made me think and question myself and I can't find any answers. That's what I've been doing these last few days; looking for answers…" another slight sob escaped her before, "I'm sorry if I've upset you, Bea. You're the most important person in the world to me really – at least you were before…" She left the sentence dangling while she pulled out a tissue and blew her nose noisily.

"Right," Beanie began in a business-like manner, "this is what you're going to do," in a tone that brooked no argument, "Put on your hat and coat and go, now, and talk to the man! He might very well be missing you too and he's almost certainly missing Sophie. The least you can do is comfort each other over that part of this situation."

Unused to being ordered about by her younger sister, Mary put on her porkpie hat and her coat and without really thinking any further about what she might be going to say to Kevin, found herself marching down the towpath to his boat.

***

She made her way through the cabin, noticing that it was unusually tidy and that even the bird-cum-dog cage had been folded and put away. The sleeping bag was no longer rolled up on the sofa and the bed in its own chamber was neatly made up in manly coloured bedsheets. The mildness of the weather meant that the stove was not lit and there were no signs of a meal having recently been prepared or eaten. The door at the far end, up to which led two large steps which doubled as storage boxes, was opened from the outside and Porkpie clambered ungracefully out into the well.

"How have you been without her?"

"Are you missing her as much as I am?"

They both spoke at the same time and then smiled at each other. The awkwardness dissipated immediately and Kevin embraced his friend in a warm hug. "Of course, I've missed her, and I've missed you too. I'm so glad you've come along this evening," and he squeezed her once more before backing away with his hands on her shoulders, looking intensely into her eyes.

Unaccustomed to such warmth in his greeting, Mary was at something of a loss as to how to continue but he could see from the expression on

186

her face that something was troubling her. "Spit it out," he suggested. At that she relaxed and pretended to spit over the side of the boat into the water; they both laughed.

"I think I've been a bit silly," she began, "after all, I'm almost old enough to be your mother, but I want you to know that I value our friendship more than you probably realise." Kevin began to speak but she held up her hand, "May I finish first?" and he nodded, "I've never really been in love and I began to think I might be in love with you because I missed you so terribly after Sophie had left and there was no special reason to see you. I expect you think I'm a silly old fool but you have become a very important person in my life." She paused, looked away into the water and then back into his eyes, "What I'm trying to say, I think, is that I want to be part of your life; to be important to you as I have been recently. Is that something that you can accept?"

Kevin took her hands and they sat down, one either side of the well, linked only by eyes and hands. "There is nothing I would like more than to have you in my life as my friend, my confidante, my soul-mate but there is something that you will need to understand and accept if our friendship is to last."

She squeezed his hand in encouragement for him to continue, "I have been a loner for most of my life," he explained, "I enjoy my own company and I don't like to be in a crowd. I'm not antisocial, there are many people whose presence I enjoy at times, but generally speaking I'm happiest alone or in a small group such as we have enjoyed over the past few days of Sophie's being here. I do miss her, and you most dreadfully and I think about you both all the time; that's why I keep so busy so that I don't have time to hurt."

Porkpie agreed completely with what he was saying; it was her philosophy too and being alone, apart from the company of her sister, was far preferable to large crowds and parties. She understood exactly what he was saying and she realised that was what she wanted for herself as well. Yes, she did love him and she did want to be with him sometimes, but it was not the sort of loving that bound them to be at each-others' side at all times.

So it was that the two 'odd-balls' formed a lasting friendship which would sustain them through good times and bad for the rest of their lives; nothing formal, no strings attached, just a meeting of hearts and minds that linked their souls in perpetuity.

A short while later, Porkpie made her way home. She smiled at her sister saying, "Thanks Bea, everything is sorted." Without further explanation, she went to bed.

Never again was this conversation spoken of or referred to; Kevin reverted to his almost monosyllabic self and Porkpie to her semi-austere and habitually upright manner, but between the two was a deep understanding and lifetime commitment. However, remembering the bird and a conversation with Sophie, whenever Porkpie and Kevin met, one or other of them would ask, "Which are you today, a rook or a crow?"

Epilogue

Sophie held tightly to the hand of her small daughter. Although she loved the water, especially where a river meandered through open fields, she remained wary of narrow towpaths and wooded areas. Some half-forgotten fears made her tighten her grip until they emerged out of the darkened coppice and from under the old stone bridge into the bright sunlight. Tall trees populated the far side of the river and in the tops of the trees, high up in the branches, were many nests. "Look up there, Lily," Sophie pointed to the treetops, "That's called a rookery. It's where the rooks make their homes and raise their babies."

Lily looked solemnly up at the silhouetted birds and their nests before the two of them continued on their stroll. As they rounded the next bend, two boys on bicycles raced past them whooping loudly in excitement and disturbing the stillness of the afternoon. As if one, the rooks flew up into the sky, cawing and calling in warning as the boys shot along the path and disappeared into the tunnel of bridge and trees.

Lily laughed delightedly at the chattering birds and watched as they gradually settled back into their roosts.

A little further along the towpath, a lone bird stood on top of a fence post. "Oh look, Mummy. One has got left behind!"

Sophie looked more closely and then knelt down beside her child. "No Lily," she said softly, "That one's not a rook. It's very similar but can you see its beak is a different colour?"

"Yes," breathed the child, "but if it's not a rook, then what is it?"

"Well, that's easy!" Sophie stood up again and with a faraway look in her eyes, she recited, "A single rook is a certain crow; but rows of crows, despite their looks, are rooks!"

Printed in Great Britain
by Amazon

35463539R00106